# Silence In The Snow

J.W. Joyner

*"The Darkness Becomes White, On A Cold Winter's Night*
*The Forest Will Freeze, As Far As The Eye Can See"*

- J.W. Joyner


March 26th, 2025

For Ethel, Ed, Brian, My Children and Grandchildren.

A leaf fell on that fall day, the first leaf of the season, in Garville, New York. The winds were light, but the smell of autumn, a sign that summer was over and Halloween was around the corner, moved through the woods. The leaf slowly shed off the maple tree, swaying in the wind, circling slowly as it fell down below, landing in a pumpkin patch.

As the leaf drifted down, it landed on a pumpkin perfectly. But this leaf began to sink into the flesh of the ripe pumpkin. As the leaf sank deeper into the pumpkin, it began emitting an orange glow. The pumpkin started to expand and contract, its glow turning brighter and brighter. Then it started to crack open like an egg; something started peering out.

The crack began to open, and what came out was covered in pumpkin guts and seeds, and then it just all fell to the ground as the pumpkin split in half. The creature flopped out of the pumpkin remains, snapping some seeds under its weight.

It had a beak, and a black body marked only with streaks of orange around its neck and chest. Its wings and eyes were orange as well. It was a crow, a black and orange crow that stood up and shook the sludge off itself. It looked around, taking in its environment. Thoughts raced through its head. *How did this come to be? What was it here for, and how did a leaf and a pumpkin create it, and why?* With a caw, the crow flew off into the sky like it had a destination, a purpose, a reason to exist.

Down in the town of Garville, the night started to fall, and the local parade was starting to begin welcoming the autumn season; all of the small shops up and down the main drag of the town were open for business, and the streets were bustling with the locals.

Mr. Thompson's candy shop was open, Mr. Grady's pizza joint was open, Old Man Johnson's liquor store was open; fire barrels on every corner were burning so the locals and visitors could keep warm. Mrs. Barnes set up her hot chocolate stall on the corner of Lansdale and Fort Rd. for everyone, only five cents a cup. The wafting aroma is irresistible to bystanders. The local kids were all dressed warm, waiting for the parade to start, knowing that candy was going to be thrown by the local fire trucks as they drove down the road.

As the night fell upon the town, the street lights began to turn on, and the parade started, beckoning the public to come and watch. Workers and customers began to come out to watch from the local businesses. A young pizza shop employee came out and stood in her uniform. Her name tag read Leeann. Fatigue marked her face; the last six hours had been grueling. She pushes her auburn hair out of her eyes.

As the parade went on and the children were catching candy, she caressed her stomach. Leeann was pregnant with her first child. She had been told she was huge for her petite frame, especially considering she had a couple more months to go. As the fire trucks went by and blew their horn, Leeann clenched her stomach and fell to the ground in pain, "Oh my God, the baby is coming," she yelled.

A local lady, Sandy, saw her and came down from the corner just a store away, "What's wrong?"

Leeann said, "I think I'm going into labor, but it's too early."

"I'm Sandy; what do you mean too early?"

"I mean, it's too early; I'm not due for another two months…" Leeann said.

Sandy thought fast, "Well, by the look of it, the baby is ready now; we need to get you to the hospital."

"But, it's too early." Leeann repeated.

Sandy helped her up and waved down the firemen. She informed the firemen of the situation and asked them for help taking her to the hospital.

Leeann kept repeating that it was too early. She couldn't think to say anything else as her heart plummeted and waves of pain traveled through her.

"Tommy, call for an ambulance, this woman is in labor," said one of the firemen helping Leeann into the fire truck.

"Ma'am, I'm John, I'm here to help." he said, holding her pale, cold hand comfortingly.

Leeann cried, "But it's 2 months too early."

John responded, "It may be, but this baby wants out now; the ambulance is on its way. Ma'am, Ma'am, stay with me, Ma'am…" as Leeann's eyes started to flicker. John urgently said, "Tommy, we need that ambulance here…" Then Leeann blacked out.

Leeann came in and out of consciousness on the ride to the hospital, "Ma'am, can you hear me, ma'am? What's your name?" John would question every time Leeann would gain consciousness.

"Leeann." she mumbled and lost conscience again throughout the ride to the hospital. She could hear everything around her, but her eyes refused to open to allow her to wake up.

When she finally woke up, she was in the hospital, and there were doctors around her. "Ma'am, Leeann, stay with us," they would urge.

Leeann weakly responded, "Yes, but it's too early."

"I'm Bruce, and you are in labor. We can't deliver the baby naturally; you're going to need an emergency C-section," he calmly explained.

Leeann began to worry, "What's wrong with the baby?"

Bruce continued calmly, trying to soothe Leeann, "The baby is fine, but we need to deliver the baby now. A C-section is the best and safest way to do it right now. Can you tell me your name, how old you are, and where you live?"

"Leeann Shanks, I'm 22, and I live at Mr. Grady's pizza joint at 22 Main Street."

Bruce smiled and continued, "It's nice to meet you, Leeann; now, let's meet your baby." As they rolled her out of the room and to the operating theatre, Leeann's glance fell to a window and she saw a black and orange crow, which was sitting on the window ledge looking at her. She was taken by surprise; she had never seen a black and orange crow, let alone one that was looking at her with orange eyes.

A wave of calm washed over her. She believed that everything was going to be okay like the baby was going to be just fine. *How could a crow have such a profound effect on her?* It seemed like the black and orange crow was a guardian angel, and she knew it was watching over her and the baby.

As Leeann lay there and the nurses prepped her for the emergency C-section, her mind kept going back to the orange and black crow and its glowing orange eyes. *Why was it there, and what purpose did it serve? Why did it seem to give her a feeling of inner peace?* She felt undeserving of it. She wasn't a saint— she had her demons.

Leeann drifted off into her thoughts, and she was snapped back to the sounds of reality. She could suddenly hear the room's noise, the nurses, the doctors, and then she heard it. "Come on, sweetheart, breathe, breathe, breathe…" Hearing those words filled her with fear. She looked into the blinding lights attached to the ceiling, a tear rolled down from her right eye, then another one from her left eye, and both tears slowly descended down her cheeks. Reality set in. *Was she going to lose her child? What is she going to do?*

Her bottom lip started to tremble, and the tears filled her eyes to a blur… The echoes of the voices, "Come on, honey, breathe, breathe, come on, breathe, baby…" the echoes became clearer and louder, her eyes now blinded by tears. Then suddenly, in her mind's eye, she saw those orange eyes; she heard a caw in the distance. *Why did she keep thinking about this crow?* Then it was heard, the baby started crying, and Leeann went from tears of fear, worry, and pain to tears of a mother crying with joy, happiness, and relief. A smile started to form, a smile that was filled with hope.

The baby continued to cry "Let it all out, honey, let it all out, baby," she could hear the nurses say. As they cleaned up the baby, the doctor came over to Leeann and said to her, "You did so well; the nurses are cleaning up the baby now. Soon, you will have your daughter in your arms."

Leeann smiled with tears still flowing down her face. "Is there anyone you need us to call?" the doctor asked.

Leeann slowly shook her head, and then she heard the nurse call to the doctor. "I'll be right back, Leeann," he said as he walked away. "Doctor, all of the baby's vitals are surprisingly good for a 2-month premature; she doesn't have any signs of being premature at all; she looks like a full-term baby. Even her weight, 7 pounds 9 ounces, is good.

Everything is perfect," the doctor looked just as surprised as the nurses but relieved yet puzzled at the same time.

He walked back over to Leeann quickly as she mumbled as loud as she could manage, "Is the baby alright, doctor?"

He looked at her, put his hand on her shoulder, and said, "Leeann, your daughter is just fine. What is her name going to be, Mom?"

Leeann couldn't help but smile, knowing that her baby was okay. Despite being 2 months early, "Frey, doctor, Frey Lee Shanks."

"What a pretty name, Leeann, beautiful name" a nurse cooed . The nurses wrapped Frey up and brought her to Leeann while she was being sewn up from the C-section surgery so she could see her. After the surgery, she was given Frey as they wheeled both to their room to rest.

About an hour passed, and Leeann started to wake up and open her eyes. As she looked up as the nurse fiddled around with her IV bag, she could see. Then, from the corner of her eye, she caught it. That black and orange crow perched on the windowsill, facing the room, just looking at her and the baby as they lay there together.

Leeann whispered, "Hello there, and who may you be?"

The crow tilted its head and cooed lightly.

"What a unique and pretty bird you are," she continued, "are you our watcher, the great protector?" The crow cawed louder and twice this time, "Thank you, sweet bird, thank you for making me feel calm and watching over me."

The crow cawed and cawed as if it were answering her. As the baby, Frey opened her eyes and looked at the crow, the crow gazed back into hers. Frey's eyes started to turn bluer, a dark, cold, frozen, frosted blue like the cleanest, brightest, deepest blue ocean. Frey then closed her eyes, and Leeann drifted back into sleep, but the crow stayed perched on that windowsill.

# Leeann's Story

Leeann was born Leeann Leona Shanks on the 29th of February in the small town of Destiny, just some 50 miles or so from Garville. She was raised by a single mother, Leona Shanks. She never knew who her father was.

Raised in a small, decrepit home, her mother worked hard to keep a roof over their heads. Leona struggled with what Leeann remembers as delusions, not violent by any means. Her mother just seemed to be running from something, paranoid that it was coming, whatever it was, to take Leeann and her away. *Away* was never explained, but Leeann would grow up as normal as most children. Her mother loved her, but she was also overly protective and scared of her for some reason. Warning Leeann that she herself would bring peace and salvation, but also, she could bring on destruction and damnation. Leona said that Leeann's choices in life would determine which one she would bring. Leeann never knew what her mother was talking about.

As she grew older and in the midst of her preteens, her mother became more watchful of Leeann but also more nervous and erratic. Leona would always be near Leeann. Even at school, she would see her mother watching from a distance.

Leona would talk to unknown things at night that were not there, telling whatever it is that "I know, Leeann would have to choose her path to that salvation." Leeann would hear her mother talking in her sleep about evil not taking her daughter, and that she would fight the demon inside Leeann's soul. Leeann became confused. Her mother's strange behavior was starting to drive a wedge between the two.

She also loved her mother very much but she also wanted to know what was going on. The more Leeann thought, the more she started to wonder who her father was. Where were her other family members? Are they still alive? She feared asking her mother these questions, not knowing how she would react. But it still made her wonder, was it only her and her mother?

By the time Leeann graduated and started working, her mother's mental health had begun to go downhill. She became more and more paranoid, erratic, and agoraphobic. Leeann would make her meals; sometimes, her mother would eat, and sometimes she would not. Leeann tried to get her mother help, but even the slightest mention of going to see a doctor or asking any questions about her family would send Leona over the edge. She would just say she didn't want to talk about it. As the days went on and the months passed, something started to happen one winter in February, just before Leeann's 21st birthday.

One night, after a long shift at work, Leeann came home to find her mother standing naked in front of the mirror, talking to herself about a child. Leeann's child. A child that was not conceived, born, or couldn't even be a possibility. Leeann was a virgin; she had no boyfriend, no friends… no life. Nothing at all.

But her mother was talking, almost whispering to the mirror as she stood there naked. Leeann could hear her mother, "Yes, I know she is with child… like you gave *me* with her. I know this child could be the one to stop the cold of the snow, the eyes of the frozen, the ghost in the winter snow fog. But she needs it fertilized with the semen of the Gods, the darkness of the cold, the blood of the ice, the burning of the snow."

Leeann couldn't understand her ramblings or what they meant. As her mother caressed the mirror, Leeann could only see the reflection of her mother and nothing more. Her mother could clearly see something. She whispered to the unseen, "Yes, my love, give it to me, so I might pass it on to her. Give me the power of the Gods, the curse of the damned, the blood of the ice, the coldness within the soul—"

"Mom!" Leeann shouted.

Her mother turned around and looked at Leeann as her eyes became white as the snow. Leeann was startled, "Mom, are you okay? What's going on? Your eyes—Mom!" she cried.

Her mom said, "Why yes darling, I am fine." She extended her hands out to her as if she wanted Leeann to give her a hug. "But darling, there is a storm outside. So white you can't see past the winter's bite."

Leeann turned her head to look out the window; it was indeed snowing so hard you couldn't see anything. When she turned around, her mother was face to face with her. Her mother's eyes were so white and her skin became so cold that she could feel the chill emanating off of her skin. Leeann mumbled in fear and sadness, "Mom…" as Leona's hand touched her stomach, going up her shirt. She raised her other hand up to her mouth and put her pointer finger up.

"Shhh, baby, shhh…," her mother began.

Leeann became paralyzed as her mother's cold hand lay on her stomach. "Shhh, you're okay, baby, I love you. Mommy will be right back." Leeann could feel a pressure in her stomach as her mother took her cold hand off her stomach and out from under her shirt, and her skin. Her mother kissed her on the forehead with her cold lips as she walked to the house door and put her hand on the knob.

Leeann still could not move, "I love you, Leeann. I will always be with you, baby." She opened the door and walked out into the cold, white air and blinding snow.

Leeann dropped to the floor as if she were freed when her mother crossed that door's threshold. The door shut as if the wind pulled it closed from the outside; Leeann ran to the door, grabbed cold knob and open it "Mom, no, Mom. Don't leave me, Mom!" she slid down the door, crying and calling for her mom. This felt like the last time she would see her mother.

Leeann awoke as the morning broke, and the nurse came in. "Hello there, sleepy head. I'm Betty, your nurse for the day; how are you and the little angel doing this morning?"

Leeann looked around as she tried to get her eyes in focus. "We are doing alright, thanks to you."

"Can I get you anything?" Betty asked politely.

"No, thank you," Leeann answered.

Betty continued, "Alright, just need to take the baby's vitals and give her a diaper change. Are you breastfeeding?"

Leeann asked, confused, "Breastfeeding?"

"Yes, the baby," Betty lovingly answered.

Leeann took a few seconds to gather her thoughts as she looked at the baby, "Yes, yes, I am."

"Okay, I will have someone in to help you with that. Is this your first time?"

Leeann responded shyly, "Yes, it is."

"Oh, no worries, it's simple. It's good for the baby and yourself," Betty offered.

"Thank you," Leeann said.

As Leeann lay there, she couldn't help but look over to the windowsill to see if the crow was still there. She could feel the baby's heartbeat sync with her own. As she focused on the morning light, the crow still sat there watching her and the baby. Leeann couldn't understand why. What was the crow there for? Why? What was its fascination with her and the baby? But yet she felt calm and safe as the crow sat there looking at them. Like a watcher, an angel, a guardian of some sort.

Then Betty walked back in and said, "Leeann, this is Nurse Nancy Smith. She is here to help you with breastfeeding the baby."

She looked down at her paperwork, "Frey, what a pretty name, Frey."

Nancy said, "Hello Leeann, how are you and Frey this morning?"

Leeann smiled and said, "We're doing okay. Thank you, Nancy."

"That's great; let's get little Miss Frey fed." Leeann nodded her head, and Nancy started showing her what to do.

Nancy said proudly, "There we go, she really is latching on," as she smiled at Leeann, and Leeann smiled back. Nancy looked at the windowsill. "Oh, my—"

Leeann looked at her, puzzled. "What is it?"

Nancy replied, "Nothing, sweetie, it's just the orange and black crow sitting on the windowsill."

Leeann questioned, "You can see it too? I thought it was just me."

"Yes, honey, I see it too," Nancy said, half snickering.

Leeann asked, "What does it mean?"

Nancy replied, "There are many stories behind it. But it is a good omen— it's a protector."

"I know, I can feel it," Leeann wondered out loud.

Nancy looked at her. "You can feel it, really? So, then the stories must be true."

Leeann became confused. "What stories?"

Nancy answered, "Nothing, honey, just know that it is a good omen."

Leeann questioned, "What for? What is the omen?"

Nancy ignored Leeann's question, "You need to get some rest, sweetheart. Just know that it is looking out for you and the baby".

Nancy knew what it meant, and she knew that with all good omens, something terrible must follow behind it. Every yin has to have an equal yang. There is no light without darkness, and vice versa. Leeann couldn't help but wonder what Nancy meant. What was the story? But she also had a baby to deal with, and the crow made her feel a sense of peace.

As the night fell upon Leeann's room, she and the baby started to doze off. The day went by in the blink of an eye. Betty soon walked back in for Frey and Leeann's nightly check-up before her shift was over.

"Hello honey, how are you and Miss Frey doing?"

Leeann yawned. "Excuse me; I'm sorry, we are doing alright. She seems tired, and to be honest, so am I."

Betty smiled, "That's understandable. Looks like you and the Frey are doing very well. Maybe tomorrow you both can go home."

Leeann looked at her with a smile and then thought to herself, *What am I going to do? Can I do this? I have nobody.* Betty seemed to catch on by the look in Leeann's eyes,

"Honey, please don't worry, you have this. You seem to be a very loving and nurturing mother; you've got this."

Leeann smiled with tears in her eyes, "I hope so."

Betty looked at her with a smile, "I know so, honey, you got this. It will all be fine, just get some sleep. The crow on the windowsill tells us so, all will be fine."

Leeann was shocked and confused. How did everyone know about this crow's story? How has she never heard of this? What was the story, and why her? She knew that the crow brought peace— she felt it. But why is this crow connected to her and the baby? What purpose did she and the baby serve to this crow? Was this her mother in another form, watching over her and the baby? If so, then why was it not seen till the baby was born? Did she just not notice it all this time? So many questions lay heavy on her mind, but nothing gave her answers. Nothing—no one— could give her the answers she needed, and frankly, she didn't know where to start.

Betty walked into the break room and saw Nancy sitting there. Both were leaving soon as their shift was almost over.

"Nancy?"

Nancy looked up from where she was sitting. She shot Betty a knowing look.

"Yes, Betty, I saw it too," Nancy faintly answered.

"So, you know?"

"Yes, Betty, I know."

"So, you know what's coming, Nancy?"

"Yes, it's just a matter of when."

Betty observed, "The black-orange crow is the first sign."

"It is, that is the first of many signs before its arrival. We have no clue when it will arrive, but we do know it is going to be soon."

Betty sighed, "Let's hope she is prepared for what's to come."

Nancy inhaled and exhaled. "Let's hope she is, she must have ties to it somehow."

Betty lifted her eyebrows up. "She must. I just don't know what they are."

Betty and Nancy both agreed that they must watch as they had for so many years, just as their ancestors had before them. But what form will it take this time, they wondered. What will it take this time from the people of Garville?

Leeann awoke to the morning sun shining in the window; she noticed that Frey's eyes were so bright in the sun that they looked almost like ice glistening in the light. She had never seen eyes like that on a child, let alone on a person. Baby Frey lay in her cot peacefully, already comfortable in her surroundings.

As Leeann lay there staring at Frey's eyes, the doctor walked in.

"How are you and the baby doing?"

"Good," Leeann replied softly.

"Well, good, I am Doctor Hammond. I'm happy to say that it looks like you and the baby are ready to go home. Is she taking to feedings?"

"Yes, she is doing very well," she said, smiling down at her daughter.

Hammond smiled, "That's good. How many times has she fed since you started?"

"Once, yesterday, I was going to try again in a few," Leeann replied.

"Alright, well, as long as she feeds today and you are feeling up to it, you both can be discharged today. Will that be okay with you?" he asked.

Leeann answered, "Yes, that would be great. But I came here by ambulance."

Hammond looked at her. "Do you have anyone you can contact?"

Leeann sighed, "I don't know many people in the area except for my boss Grady. He owns the pizza joint in town."

Hammond looked at his papers. "Oh, wait a minute. There is a contact for a lady named Sandy who left her number."

Leeann had to think about it for a moment, "Oh, that's the lady who helped me during the parade when I went into labor. She left a number?"

Hammond, "She left it with the ambulance paramedics. Is she okay to contact?"

Leeann responded with a low voice, "Yes, I guess. I just met her that night, but I guess it's alright."

Hammond smiled at Leeann, "Great, we will give her a call once you get the baby fed. Alright?"

Leeann nodded. Hammond walked out to give her some privacy so she could get the baby to latch and feed her.

As the morning became afternoon and the evening started to fall upon the town, Leeann became more and more anxious and wanted to just get home. Nurses had come in and checked on her and the baby throughout the day. Everything seemed to be alright. As Leeann lay there waiting to find out if she and the baby were going to leave, she couldn't help but wonder how she would do this alone. Could she raise the baby alone and be a good mother? She had no one, no family, no friends, really. She came to this town with nothing.

As she got deeper into her own head, she was startled a bit when Dr. Hammond walked in.

"Leeann, how are you and the baby doing?"

Leeann looked at him. "We are doing okay."

Hammond smiled, "Good, very good. Well, it looks like you are all set. Your discharge papers are being processed as we speak."

Leeann was happy but also worried at the same time. Just then, Sandy walked in.

Sandy smiled at Leeann and the baby, "Hello, honey. How are you? And who is this precious little one?"

Leeann beamed, "I'm okay. This is Frey."

Sandy was so smitten, smiles and all, "She is so beautiful! Look at those eyes, so bright, so pretty". Leeann smiled and was happy to have someone to lean on for now.

Sandy asked, "So, are we ready to get out of here and get you and little Frey home?"

Leeann smiled, "Yes, we are." But Leeann had that fear, that worry, in her voice.

Sandy caught on to it, "Is everything alright?" She asked as she sat on the chair next to Leeann's bed.

"I'm a bit scared. I have no one here in town…" she confessed.

Sandy stopped her mid-sentence, "There's no reason to be scared, honey. You have me; I am here to help. So is Mr. Grady and so many others in town. There is no need to worry. We have you covered."

Leeann started to tear up. "Thank you so much. Thank you"

Sandy warmly smiled, "No worries, Leeann. This town is like a family. You are a part of that family, and so is Frey. We help each other out."

The tears began to run down Leeann's face. "I can't thank you enough."

Sandy smiled as the discharge papers were handed to Leeann to sign by a young nurse.

During the ride home, Sandy and Leeann talked. Leeann knew that, eventually, she was going to be asked questions about her past and where she was from. But it wasn't going to be tonight. They talked about the baby, how working for Mr. Grady was, and how Mr. Grady and some of the people in the town got together to get her some baby clothes, a bassinet, some bottles, and some other things to help Leeann's transition to being a single mother easier. Leeann felt nothing but gratitude and relief that she had so much help. How many people cared for her in the short amount of time that she has lived in the town?

As they pulled up to Mr. Grady's pizza shop, Mr. Grady came out to meet Leeann at the car door. "There you are, Leeann, and who is this little beauty?"

"This is Frey," Leeann answered.

Grady smiled, "Well, it's nice to meet you, Frey. I'm your uncle, Grady."

Leeann was a little taken aback.

Grady asked quickly, "Is that okay?". His face turned red with embarrassment.

She smiled, "Yes, and thank you, Mr. Grady."

Grady smiled and nodded his head.

"Well, let's get you ladies inside and upstairs."

As they walked into Leeann's apartment, she was stunned to see all they had done for her. The house was cleaned, and the baby had a bassinet, diapers, a changing table, wipes, and clothes. There were even balloons that read "Welcome Little One", and so much more.

Leeann was so overjoyed that she started to cry.

"Now, now, Leeann. It's ok. We got you what you needed, hoping you wouldn't mind. Remember, we are a family in this town," Sandy proclaimed.

"I know, and no, I don't mind. I'm just so thankful for everything. I can't ever repay you all for what you are doing for us." Leeann replied with gratitude pouring out of each word.

Grady put his hand on her shoulder. "There is nothing to thank us for and nothing to repay. You are with family now."

"Thank you" is all Leeann could say. "Thank you."

As Sandy and Grady helped her get settled in and the baby down to sleep, Leeann thought about how she ended up here in this town. *Why was she in this town, and why did her car break down here?* Something didn't sit well with her.

# Leeann's Story

## Part 2

After she calmed down and realized she was never going to see her mother again, Leeann had to open the door. She could see nothing; the snow was too dense, too blinding. *How can Mom just walk out in this blizzard? How could she walk in it naked and not freeze to death?*

Something told her that her mother was gone forever, but she still had to make a missing persons report. Who would even believe her story? How could she even begin to explain what she saw?

But she had to call.

That night, reports were pouring into the station—missing cats, missing dogs, power outages, missing people—so much was happening during the storm that the police were overwhelmed and powerless to help until it finally passed.

The next day, the town started to dig out, and the police started looking for the missing animals and people. Leeann hadn't slept a wink; she didn't understand what her mother meant by all she said. Why she did what she did and what it all meant. Days turned into weeks, and then months, and nothing of her mother was found; it's like she vanished. Snow melted, and spring was about to bloom, but her mother was never found. Leeann started to make peace with what happened.

It was around this time that her health became unstable. She started experiencing recurring nausea, so she decided to get a checkup. She had never been with a man, so she knew there wasn't a possibility of being pregnant, even though she had missed her period for 2 months in a row.

She had some blood drawn as part of her check-up and was shocked when the doctors told her she was with child. How could this be? She asked the doctors to run the tests again because there was no way that she was pregnant. *There was no way, none, she was a virgin.* But she also had a feeling in her stomach; she knew something was growing in her, she could feel it.

After settling on that her mother was gone, and she had nobody to bury, Leeann decided with this new news of being pregnant, that she needed to leave, leave this all behind, and start new. But she had no idea where she was going. With a bit of money and a beat-up old car, she made up her mind to sell what she could and leave. All she knew was that she had to get out—start fresh somewhere she wasn't known, somewhere she didn't have to answer so many questions.

So, she did just that. She got in her car with some things to tide her over, such as clothes and such, and started driving from town to town and county to county, keeping the past in the rearview.

Within a week, Leeann ended up breaking down in Garville just outside Mr. Grady's pizza joint. She looked over into the pizza joint's window, and saw a "Help Wanted" sign, right under it, which said *"apartment for rent"*.

This felt like a sign from above. She got out of her beaten-down old Dodge and walked in to the pizza shop

"Hello, there young lady" a man greeted her as she walked in.

Leeann "Hello."

"What can I get for you?" the man asked.

"I'm new to the town.", replied Leeann. "My car just broke down outside your shop, and I was wondering if I could get an interview? It says you're hiring and you have an apartment for rent?"

The man looked at her and said with his hand extended out, "I'm Mr. Grady. I run this pizza joint, and you are?"

"My name is Leeann."

Mr. Grady said, "Well, nice to meet you, Leeann. " They shook hands. "You know what? You're hired."

Leeann looked surprised. "Really, that quick? No questions?"

Mr. Grady said, "Look, you seem like an honest young woman. Plus, it's only me here, and I need all the help I can get. The apartment is a small one-bedroom, one-bathroom, and it's yours as long as you are working here."

Leeann smiled, "Thank you, thank you."

Mr. Grady glanced at her car and said, "Do you have anything to bring in?"

"Just some clothes."

Mr. Grady looked puzzled. But he thought no mind of it.

"Well, that's okay. We have some furniture, a fridge, and a stove we can bring over and get you settled in."

Leeann looked surprised. "Are you sure? I have some money."

Mr. Grady waved his hand dismissively. "It's fine, let's get you settled in. When can you start?"

"ASAP", Leeann replied, a little too quickly.

Mr. Grady: "Okay, so tomorrow, good?"

Leeann smiled and replied, "Thank you, and yes".

Every day, Sandy and Grady were checking up on Leeann until she was healed enough to start working again. There was always constant help for her. She felt like she had a family, the kind of family she had lost.

From time to time, Leeann would glance at the tree outside her window. But there was no sign of the black and orange crow. *Was it just there to watch at the hospital? Was it a place that only dwelt, and why did it only seem to watch Leeann?* Maybe it was the room, maybe like a ghost; it is only drawn to one place, one room. For whatever reason, the crow seemed to have disappeared. Sometimes Leeann would feel a little silly placing so much value on a chance encounter.

But other peculiar things began happening around her. Frey's eyes seemed to be changing color. They became darker, more normal-looking since she returned from the hospital. *Was that also linked to the crow?*

Leeann started work earlier than anticipated—she needed a sense of normalcy. With Sandy's continued support, she would be able to get back on her feet.

As the month passed and bow season came to a close, with shotgun season just around the corner, she knew the pizza joint was about to get slammed with orders. Moreover, the town was in preparation for its Christmas decorations and parade.

The days were getting colder. Winter was around the corner, and Thanksgiving was just about here Christmas was around the corner, and shoppers were about to be all over town.

The first real cold started in the early morning just before Thanksgiving, the weather reports were calling for 40-mile sustained winds with 50 to 60-mile-an-hour wind gusts. The first real snowfall was about to begin tonight, not a lot, but just enough to coat the ground.

Leeann was closing the pizza joint and was about to go upstairs to help Sandy care for the baby. Then the two ladies would try and get some much-needed rest. Thanksgiving was the next day, and it was just going to be her and Frey hunkered down as the winds picked up.

Sandy greeted Leeann with a warm smile, "Hey you, how was your night?"

Leeann let out a sigh, pouring herself a glass of water, "Busy."

"Oh, I'm sorry.", Sandy said, empathizing with the new mom. "At least Frey is clean, fed, and ready for bed!"

"Sandy, you are a lifesaver; I could never repay you for all you do for Frey and me."

Sandy, placed an assuring hand on her shoulder and said, "Don't mention it. I love you too, as if you were my own blood. You're like the daughter I wished I had, and Frey is like the granddaughter I always wanted. By the way, what are you doing for Thanksgiving tomorrow?"

"Just sitting here with Frey for the night. Maybe binge watch some shows", Leeann replied.

Sandy looked down at the ground. "Hey, why don't I bring some stuff over and we can cook and have dinner together? We can hang out, watch a movie or two?"

Leeann smiled, "That would be awesome. You don't have plans?"

"Well, now I hopefully do HA-HA. So...?" she continued, eagerly.

Leeann "Yes, definitely. Thank you".

On Thanksgiving morning, Jack and his buddy Tom got up early to get out in the woods, settle in their blind, and wait for the buck they had seen from the deer-cam for the last month. 10 points, what a rack and a monster ass buck. They put on their orange camo, grabbed hand warmers, and headed out to their old F-150, then up the mountain they went. It was still pitch black.

Jack said, with enthusiasm, "Man, this is our year. Got to get that 10 pointer."

"Hell yeah, man. We're going to get it, I just know it, brother," replied Tom. As they drove up the blistery hill on the dirt road, the wind was brutal.

Jack continued, "Man, this wind has blown so hard. All of the leaves on the trees are just flying everywhere."

Tom: "Yeah, man, the ground is going to be covered. It's going to be hard to track anything we might hit, man. I hope there is some snow that's going to stick, makes it easier to track blood trails and deer tracks".

"Man, isn't that the truth?"

As Jack and Tom pulled up to the side of the road Tom "Shit, man."

"What?" Jack asked.

Tom replied, "I forgot the apples, man."

Jack "Shit. Well, what do we have?"

"I'll have to take a look. We have the salt lick down below the old oak tree, and I'll see what I have in the back of the truck bed".

As they got out of the truck, the wind grew stronger and stronger.

Tom opened up the tailgate and flashed his light inside "Shit man, all I have is an old rotting pumpkin from Halloween. Do deer eat that?"

Jack added, "I don't know, man, let's take it anyway."

Tom agreed, and they took the pumpkin with them. Tacking through the woods with their headlamps on, walking to their blind.

"Man, I hope the blinds are still standing," said Tom.

"It should be, buddy. I just hope the heaters are still working. I know we still have those three propane tanks up there," Jack said.

"Yeah, we haven't really used them yet this year, so we should be all good, man," Tom replied.

As they walked up to the blind, they noticed it was still standing.

"Dude, awesome—it's still standing," Jack said excitedly.

"Hell yeah it is. Hey, where should we put the pumpkin?"

Jack looked around with his light. "Let's put it under the maple tree—the one with the single leaf on it."

"Sounds good, man. Maybe the buck will go for the leaf and notice the pumpkin."

"Maybe, man. Maybe."

Tom laid the pumpkin down underneath the maple tree while Jack got the heater going.

As they got warm and comfortable, Tom could see a light in the distance, not so deep within the woods.

Tom tapped Jack's arm and pointed. "What's that man?"

Jack looked over to where Tom was pointing. "I don't know. But it looks like a lit lantern."

"Maybe it's the old hermit that they say lives in these here woods."

"Man, I thought he was a myth."

"I guess not. But hey, maybe it's the game warden."

"I don't think so. They would use a flashlight, I would think."

"I don't know, man."

As they sat there watching, they could see the lantern moving around in the distance.

Tom finally spoke, "Man, I hope they don't scare the big buck off."

"You know, I hope they don't. But then again, they may kick it up to us," pondered Jack.

"True man, true."

As the dawn became closer and the sky became a little brighter, Jack heard the rustling of leaves on his right.

"Did you hear that?" he whispered

"Yeah." Tom whispered. They kept their eyes peeled and looked around through the window of their blind, and there just over the side ridge came the buck they had been waiting for. The buck walked over to the pumpkin under the maple tree and started sniffing around.

Tom and Jack were shocked and amazed by the sheer size of the buck.

Jack nudged Tom, "Man, take the shot," Jack whispered

Tom, still uncertain, asked, "Are you sure, man?"

Jack whispered back, "Take the shot."

Tom lifted his rifle, aimed, just as a big gust of wind blew, knocking the maple leaf out of the tree. As it floated down, Tom took the shot.

*BANG!*

Right through the heart. As the deer dropped down, the leaf hit the rotting pumpkin just as the blood hit it, the shot echoed through the woods.

Jack "Holy shit, man! You got it!"

As they got out of the blind, celebrating their kill, the hermit came running up and stopped dropping the lantern to the ground and then to his knees.

Hermit yelled, "No, no! What have you *done*?" He cried out.

Jack and Tom stared at him. "What?" Tom asked confused

The hermit pointed to the pumpkin, shaking from the cold, and Jack and Tom looked to where he was pointing. The blood on the pumpkin seemed to seep into the pumpkin's rotting skin, as did the leaf.

Tom and Jack looked on in fear and amazement. "What the…?" Tom's voice trailed. The pumpkin began to pulsate, as if it were breathing, and its glow intensified from within.

You could see something growing in it. You could see the pumpkin guts, almost like veins inside, moving slowly around. Then it became silent; the wind had stopped blowing, and a cold calmness started to settle in the air.

Hermit's voice shook, "Oh my God."

Jack and Tom asked, "What?"

The pumpkin began to show signs of something emerging from within as it cracked and started to hatch, much like an egg. The guts started to ooze out, and old and dark, almost black blood started to trickle out of it. Then it happened: a black crow with blood-red eyes crawled out. The hermit, Jack, and Tom stared in a trance-like state. The crow looked at them all and cawed with a blood-drenched sound and flew off into the night sky.

The wind started to pick up, and the snow began to blow in. "What the hell *was* that?" Jack asked, looking at the hermit. The hermit covered his face with his cold hands and shook his head back and forth.

"Dude, what the fuck was that?" Tom damn near shouted while looking at the hermit. The hermit kept his hands on his face and kept shaking his head from side to side.

Jack kneeled down to the hermit and put his hand on his shoulder and whispered, "Man, what was that? What the hell just happened?"

The hermit lifted his head up and his eyes, blue as blue and bright as ice with frozen tears pouring out of his eyes". It is the second sign. It is coming, and it is coming soon to collect on this town".

Jack asked, "What is coming? What is it called? What does it want? What is it here to collect?"

Tom replied, "Yeah man, what?"

The hermit glared at them both "It is coming to bring the cold of winter, the freeze of ice, the death of souls, the hunger it needs. The darkness will fall upon us, and the winter will be as blinding as a blizzard, and within it will walk the monster of death as it feeds on this town".

Jack looked at him like he was nuts, a loon "What is it, old man?"

Jack shook him and the hermit whispered "Evil Pure, cold, black, evil". As the old man stood up, he picked up his lantern, and began to walk away.

"Wait what, old man?", Jack stumbled over his words.

"Never mind him man, he's crazy", Tom shrugged. "Let's get the deer gutted on the truck, and get out of here"

Jack was confused "But Tom, we have never seen nothing like that before. Dude, a crow just came out of a fucking pumpkin!"

"I know man; I just want to get our deer and get out of here. If you want, we can gut it at the truck", was the hurried reply.

Jack agreed to gut the deer there, and they got to work. They loaded it in the back of the truck bed and got the hell out of there.

As the morning was about to break. Frey started to wake up crying. The wind outside was still blowing hard, rattling the windows throughout the house. Frey had never cried like this before, it was unusual to Leeann. It was the first time since Frey was born that she had woken Leeann from a deep sleep. Leeann walked over to the bassinet and saw Frey's face was flushed.

As she reached down to touch her, she could feel the heat radiating off of her. She was running a fever. Frey was also wet and needed a diaper change, but she was also clammy and drenched in sweat. As Leeann picked her up and put her on the bed to change her and take her temperature, the first light of day began to slip through the window curtains. Then she heard a big bang in the distance, it was a gunshot, and the wind then just stopped blowing. Startled, Leeann took a few steps toward the window and pulled the curtains open to look outside.

Frey had just suddenly stopped crying. Leeann then looked away from the window and looked down at Frey lying on the bed, and could tell something was wrong. Leeann rushed over to check on Frey. Frey took a deep breath in and slowly exhaled—and the air that left her lips was ice cold. She stared straight ahead, eyes wide and unblinking, as if caught in a trance. Leeann touched her skin; it was still burning with fever. But that breath—so cold it seemed to freeze the air around them. A chill ran through Leeann's body, and she watched as frost began to creep across the windowpane.

Leeann looked at the window and the room as it felt like the temperature had dropped 20 degrees from one exhale from Frey's lungs. Leeann looked back down at Frey, the child was staring up and to the left. Her breathing was shallow, and she was twitching slightly.

"Frey, baby?" Leeann cried out in fear. Frey didn't respond. "Frey, Frey!" Leeann yelled, tears welling in her eyes. She picked up the infant in her arms and began to swing her. Nothing changed. Frey continued to feel feverous, her breath cold as ice, still slightly twitching on and off.

As Leeann rushed to Frey, she clutched her tightly, scrambling around the room with one hand, searching for her phone to call 911. "Frey, baby—Frey! Stay with me, FREY!" she cried out, her voice breaking. Tears blurred her vision as panic overtook her. But then, through the blur, she glanced out the window—and froze.

Though tears clouded her vision, Leeann could see a winged creature in the distance flying toward the window, but she couldn't make out what it was. The air became thick, cold, and Leeann could barely breathe; it was like she was being smothered, and her lungs were freezing from the inside out. Time seemed to freeze as something flew straight toward the window, heading for them both. Leeann's body was paralyzed—she couldn't move, couldn't speak. Only her eyes shifted, wide with fear.

Frey was still twitching and warm to the touch, and Leeann couldn't do anything. She stood helpless, paralyzed. Frey's eyes rolled into the back of her head as she began to twitch more and more, her eyelids started twitching as the winged object flying got closer and closer to the window.

Leeann began to fear that she was going to lose Frey. She couldn't move, she couldn't get to her phone to call for help, she was helpless, and she was scared. Then she whispered, "Frey," barely being able to move her mouth.

Then Frey's eyes became straight forward, eyelids wide open, the twitching stopped, and Frey's eyes started to change color slowly. Leeann's eyes couldn't help but move to look at the window, like they were forced to look.

Leeann's eyes slowly began to clear, the haze lifting as her focus sharpened. The shape outside came into view, becoming more distinct as it landed on the windowsill. It was the black and orange crow. Leeann felt like she could move again as it landed on the windowsill, and she looked immediately down to Frey and noticed her eyes had changed back to that more blue, that dark, cold, frozen frosted blue. The color she had when she was born.

Frey's body started to cool down, and the apartment started to warm up again. Frey took a deep breath in and then out, and it was a normal temperature again. Leeann was amazed and just held Frey in her arms, with tears rolling down her face. She held Frey's head tight against her shoulder, facing the window. As the wind started to pick up again, the snow started to fly. Frey looked at the crow as the crow looked at her, eyes locked with each other.

Through the wind and snow, the black crow glided above the leafless trees, its blood-red eyes scanning left to right, as if searching the ground below. Then, suddenly, its gaze locked—like it had found what it was looking for through the swirling snow. Without hesitation, the crow swooped down into the dense forest, landing on an old concrete foundation. The structure was cracked and weathered, covered in patches of moss, ice, and snow.

The foundation had been sitting deep in the woods for years, untouched by the world around it; nothing but nature had disturbed it. The black crow cawed loudly as it echoed throughout the dense, cold woods, and then it flew down to the center of the foundation and cawed into the air. The black crow started to peck at the ground through the snow, ice, and dirt.

As its beak hit the concrete below, it cracked, and it continued to peck through as if it were a jackhammer breaking through the old concrete. The crow peaked and peaked more intensely, harder and harder, as lightning started to fill the sky above. Though the wind and the snow, the clouds began to turn in the air as the lightning bolts streaked through the sky. The rotting concrete cracked more as the crow hit harder and harder. As the concrete gave way more and more, and the dirt below started to become more exposed, black liquid started to ooze out of the ground like thick oil, like syrup from a tree, thick and slow running.

The lightning became more intense, and the wind blew even stronger. The snow became more blinding, and the clouds circled faster and faster, raging more and more out of control. The dim light of the morning sky became darker and covered by the dark shadow of the snow, which became heavier, and the wind was blowing it like a force from Hell.

The crow lifted its head to the sky and let out a single, piercing caw—more a shriek than a call, almost like a scream. Then it flew to the edge of the foundation wall and cried out again, over and over, each caw louder and more urgent than the last. From the ground beneath, a thick, black syrup-like liquid began to seep more aggressively, and the earth itself started to pulse, as if straining to give birth to something hidden deep within. The ground bled darkness. The crow screamed. The wind howled. Lightning tore across the sky as the clouds twisted and circled, casting deeper shadows over the land. Slowly, droplets of the black liquid began to rise from the soil, suspended in the air. Time seemed to slow, the storm growing more violent, pounding the world with relentless, brute force.

The black crow let out a loud, painful caw, and the black liquid started to rise more and more until it shot up like a bullet into the air. As the swirling clouds opened up around the liquid, it became a circular vortex as it curved like a rainbow above the clouds and into the distance, where no man has ever walked or has ever been. The Blacklands, as it's called, where nothing treads, nothing living has been there, and nobody dares to go. The black liquid started to form a large growing circle pushing the clouds circling it farther apart, spinning to the left slowly as it picked up speed. The black crow continued to caw relentlessly as the swirling black liquid spun faster, twisting into a tornado-like column. Then, a bolt of lightning struck the liquid with a violent crack—like a jolt of electricity, charging it, feeding it, giving it life.

Then the lightning just stopped, and the liquid tube started to slow down to a stop. It was suspended in the air with the clouds around it, stopping as well. The wind died down, and the snow slowed to almost nothing. The crow stopped cawing, but its head was still pointed to the sky. The black crow followed with its head and blood red eyes, the last snowflake to hit the ground.

The column of black liquid began to spin slowly to the right, gradually gaining speed. Above it, the clouds responded—churning in the same direction, drawn into the motion like they were tethered to the swirling darkness below.

The lightning started to feed into the liquid tube again as the wind started to blow more intensely, and the snow began again, thicker and harder. The crow lifted its beak toward the sky and let out a loud, piercing caw. Suddenly, the black liquid fell from above, raining down onto the ground below. The clouds closed in and ceased their spinning; the lightning stopped streaking across the sky, no longer feeding the dark column.

The black crow followed the last of the black liquid down as it hit the ground. The black liquid started to seep into the ground where it once came, like the dry cracking dirt devours the rain as it needs its moisture to heal its cracks and become alive again.

Leeann couldn't believe what had just happened. She couldn't understand why the black and orange crow had vanished and then returned—or what connection it had to her, especially to Frey. Still shaken by the strange events, she grabbed her phone and quickly texted Sandy…

*"Hey, Sandy, something happened. Are you awake?"* Leeann typed shakily.

A few minutes passed by as Leeann paced the floor impatiently. Frey continued to keep her eyes locked on the crow's eyes and the crow's eyes locked on hers.

Sandy's message popped up on the screen: *"Hey, honey, what's going on?"*

Leeann: *"Frey had some sort of a seizure, I think. I'm not sure."*

Sandy: *"My God, is she alright? What happened?"*

Leeann: *"She's alright, I think. I can explain it when I see you. I'm so sorry to text this early in the morning, but I don't know what to do."*

Sandy: *"I'm on my way."*

Leeann paced nervously, waiting for Sandy to arrive. Frey seemed okay, but Leeann could feel her body growing hotter—something wasn't right. Tears welled up as she whispered, "Honey, you'll be alright. Please, God, be alright." The black and orange crow turned away from the window, its gaze sweeping across the snowy, wind-swept land.

Then Frey's breathing grew shallow. The crow let out a piercing, screaming caw. Frey's head tilted back, her eyes rolling upward again. Leeann gently lifted her from her shoulder, holding her close. "Frey, honey, oh my God, Frey!" she pleaded, panic rising. The crow's caw echoed like a scream, the wind howled louder, and snow slammed against the windowpane. Leeann sobbed, clutching Frey tight, begging, "Please, baby, please, honey—don't leave me. Don't do this!"

Then a knock at the door, "Leeann?", it was Sandy's voice; Leeann put Frey to her shoulder again and walked quickly to the door to unlock it for Sandy "Sandy, it's happening again, I don't want to lose her, what do, I do?"

Sandy urged, "Give her to me."

Leeann handed Frey to Sandy and started to pace around the room crying and shaking, Sandy holding Frey looked at her "Frey, honey its ok, Frey come back, Frey". Sandy could hear the black and orange crow cawing from the windowsill, the sound piercing her ears.

Leeann went to the window and began shouting, "WHAT DO YOU WANT FROM US? WHY ARE YOU DOING THIS TO HER? WHAT ARE YOU, LEAVE HER BE!!!"

Sandy laid Frey on the bed and kept whispering in her ear, "Frey, honey, come back to us. Frey?"

The black and orange crow cawed louder and louder, looking into the white lands, out into the blinding snow.

Leeann put her hand on the window and begged, "Please, please don't take her from me. Please don't do this, let her be."

The black and orange crow, with the wind blowing stronger, though its feathers, slowly turned its head and gazed into Leeann's eyes. Leeann suddenly felt a wave of calm wash over her. It seemed to communicate with her through its gaze into her eyes. Leeann couldn't look away. She could hear Sandy talking to Frey, but it sounded muffled and distant. So was the crow's cawing. Though it continued to caw loudly as it stared into Leeann's eyes, it was like it was far away.

Then, as Leeann looked deeper into its eyes, it all started to unfold. She could see a black spiral, frozen children, a dark hooded figure, a land buried in dirt, a well of creatures surrounded by blood and corpses, bones of the lost, pain of the forgotten. A place where life and death seem to collide with evil. Leeann couldn't understand the flashes of what she was seeing; she couldn't grasp it all. At the same time, she could feel peace and fear as she knew something was coming. What it was she didn't know, but she knew something was coming for her and for Frey.

"Leeann, Leeann," she could hear the voice coming closer as Sandy put her hand on Leeann's shoulder. Then the black and orange crow's caws became louder, and every sound slowly became normal again. Leeann snapped out of it as the black and orange crow looked back out into the wind and snow.

"Sandy, she will be alright."

"I'm calling 911", Sandy said.

"No, just wait", Leeann said in a low voice

Sandy was confused by the calmness of Leeann's tone. "But she's having a seizure, Leeann. And she isn't coming out of it."

"Just wait," as she took Sandy's hands in hers.

Leeann's hands were so cold, but Sandy suddenly felt calm and at peace, just like Leeann did when she stared at the black, orange crow's eyes. Then, the black and orange crow stopped cawing and turned back to looking in the window.

Leeann said, "Look," and Sandy turned to the bed, and Frey was alright, looking at them both.

Sandy was confused by what had just transpired; She looked at Leeann as "What just happened?"

"I don't know Sandy. But I do know it was going to be alright."

"How Leeann, how?"

"I just do," Leeann said. "I just do."

Betty woke up to hear the sound she had dreaded for years. She knew that it was coming, but she didn't know when. She knew that Leeann and baby Frey were the first signs of it. Betty rolled over in bed and looked at her phone lying on her nightstand. As she reached for it, she knew that there would be a text. She picked it up off the nightstand and slowly looked at it…

*"You know what that sound meant?"* Nancy inquired.

*"Yes, I do, Nancy"*, Betty replied somberly.

*"It's coming. Now the second sign of the caws was the warnings of its coming."*

*"I know it was, Nancy."*

*"We can only hope for the best, we can only hope that the baby is the chosen one to fight it and stop its reign of pain and terror. We have lost so much over time."*

*"I know, and we know that it's going to bring the winter blizzard with it—the wind, the zero cold chills, and it's coming for the children. And it's coming for us,"* said Betty.

*"Yes, I know we need to prepare for it. It knows we have what it needs."*

*"Yes, we do, Nancy, we need to let it go."*

*"What form do you think it will take? Who's the last soul that was lost? Who will it be?"*

"I don't know, but it must have some ties to Leeann and the baby *Frey*", Betty pondered.

*"Do you think she knows?"* Nancy replied inquisitively.

*"By now, she should know something."*

*"God, I hope so"*

*"So do I, Nancy, so do I."*


Betty took in a deep breath and set her phone back on the nightstand and lay back down, looking up at the ceiling. She knew that whatever was coming, she had a fight on her hands, and it would come for Nancy and her with a vengeance.

As the black crow stood on the foundation wall, its blood red eyes stared down at the floor where it pecked so intensely to release the black liquid from the ground. As it stared, the ground started to slowly seep out the black liquid that it had swallowed up. The black liquid oozed out in a thin layer, covering the dirt below. Then, it started to boil, and hot steam began to rise from it.

The crow fixed its gaze upon it, blood-red eyes welling with crimson tears that streaked down its obsidian feathers and dripped from its beak. Beneath the black, seething liquid, the ground began to throb, like living flesh crawling beneath the surface.

As a hand started to come out of its cover, in the black ooze forming around it like skin. Every crease in its hand, every detail, every mark, every line. The black crow watched as it formed, then another hand formed, pushing up from the ground. Both hands grabbed the broken concrete around the dirt and pulled itself out. A head started to push up from the ground below. The black liquid forming around it revealed every detail on its face, with its long white hair starting to take shape as the black liquid revealed more detail. Its mouth opened as the liquid started to run down its throat.

The torso and breasts started to form as the liquid wrapped around its chest, showing its nipples and stomach.

It kept pulling itself out of the liquid, its hips and rear started to show along with its genitalia as the liquid ran inside of it and down its legs until it came fully out of the ground and stood up. It let out a screeching banshee scream.

As it stood there naked in the snow, the black liquid stopped boiling and tightened to its feminine form. She opened her eyes, and you could see the blackness where her eyes should be. The black crow's tears, now blood, ran down its beak. The crow took flight with a caw and perched upon it, as she walked into the wind, blowing snow naked through the woodlands, the black crow guiding it with its eyes.

The old hermit opened the door to his house, closing it behind him. As the cold swept through before it shut, knowing that it was coming. He knew when the two hunters shot that deer and the blood hit the rotting pumpkin as the leaf fell on it, that the black crow was going to be born. Bringing upon the world the only thing that could resurrect it. It was a matter of time before it was going to rise from its slumber, and he knew he had to prepare for its arrival. He also knew that the black and orange crow was born with the first leaf that fell at the beginning of the fall season from the first fully developed pumpkin.

He knew there was hope for the children, but not for himself, nor for anything that stood in its way. The hermit wanted revenge for what it had taken from him long ago— what cursed him, keeping him alive all these years. He would stand up to it. Revenge was all he desired for the loss of his only daughter. He knew he held the cloth it wanted, the one it needed, and he had hidden it, waiting for its return.

The hermit couldn't help but close his eyes and think back to that cold winter night. The snow was blowing, and the wind had picked up. Many of the town's children had disappeared, and the hermit kept a close eye on his little girl as she slept in her bed. He lay down next to his little girl and dozed off.

As he slept, a cold whistling breeze started to fill the room, and he woke up when he heard what sounded like the house door rattle furiously, as if something was trying to get in. He thought nothing of it, thinking it was the wind, but it became more furious. He slowly moved his arm from underneath his daughter, careful not to wake her, and went to check the door. He walked out of the room, looked back at her, shut the door, leaving it open just a crack, and walked into the living room. He could see the door was closed but rattling, but he could swear that he had locked it tight before they had lain down to sleep.

As he walked back toward his daughter's bedroom, he could see that the wood in the fireplace was getting low, so he stoked the fire before he headed back into her bedroom. As he stoked the fire, he felt the cold breeze coming from his daughter's room. As he stood up from stoking the fire, he heard a tapping on his windowsill, and he looked toward it. There stood a blood-red-eyed crow, staring back at him. He felt a chill as he looked into the black crow's eyes; he knew something wasn't right. He turned his attention back to his daughter's room, where the cold breeze had been coming from, and slowly opened the door.

Standing there was a person, leaning over his daughter, wearing a dark, cloaked garment. "Who are you?" He asked in shock, "What are you doing in my daughter's room?" The person never moved their head, but they pointed at him with their left hand, and he stood there unable to move. All he could do was watch in fear of what this thing, person, was going to do to his daughter. As this thing stood there, it reached down and touched the little girl's face with its other hand; the little girl whimpered in her sleep with its cold touch.

He could see the cold steam rising from its hands as it touched his daughter's face, and could see that her face had frost on it. As it caressed her cheek, she started to wake up; he knew one of them was losing their life. As she woke up and slowly opened her eyes, she wanted to scream 'no,' but couldn't.

As his daughter opened her eyes and looked, she could see the cold blackness of its eyes looking back at her, and she was about to scream, but its cold eyes hypnotized her. Its eyes started to fog as the little girl lay there frozen in its gaze. Then, like a snow globe, it started to snow within the blackness of its eyes. Its chest started to glow red. He could only watch in fear, the little girl started to rise up off her bed. Her skin became cold and pale, and then it forced her down to a standing position. It lowered its left hand and, with both hands, it grabbed the little girl's shoulders.

He became unparalyzed and shouted "No!" before starting to run to his daughter's side. As he did, he grabbed its dark, cloth cloak and tore it from the creature holding his daughter. It broke eye contact with his daughter's eyes and snarled at him as the crow let out a screeching caw. The windows throughout the house shattered. As the cold winds collided with the creature in the bedroom, it raised its head into the air, and the winds spiraled around it like a tornado; it disappeared within its tight grasp.

He dropped the dark cloth cloak as his daughter fell lifeless to the ground, and he caught her, sobbing. "Baby, wake up, please, honey, don't go, I can't lose you too, baby, please".

The little girl could only whisper as she took her last breath, "Daddy, Daddy, I'm so cold."

"It's okay, baby, Daddy's here". As his tears ran down his face, he had no choice but to watch and feel the life within his little girl drift out of her. All he could do was hold her and not let her body hit the floor.

As he sat in his rocking chair by the lit fireplace, he waited to hear its scream. The crows cried out—harsh, piercing caws—and he knew the birth was beginning. He waited, but she would come for him first, to take the cloth. He knew it. It needed the cloth after its birth.

Then came the scream—banshee-like, sharp, and near. It was here, coming for him. The wind howled louder, snow slammed the windows, and the cold crept through the old wooden boards, rattling them as its presence inched closer. He waited.

Then he felt it—just beyond the door. The fire blazed, but his breath turned to mist. The warmth faded as the door rattled, ice creeping over it. The cold became bone-deep. The hermit could hardly breathe—his lungs freezing with each shallow gasp.

It stood outside the door and put its hand on it, turning the wood to ice and glass as it shattered. The hermit felt the cold and the ice fly past him; he stayed seated in his chair, waiting for its approach with his eyes closed. It walked in as the crow's eyes scanned the room. The crow cawed and flew off its shoulder, flying around the room cawing more and more. Then it landed on the mantel above the fireplace, staring down at the old hermit. It walked toward him and laid its hands on the back of his old chair. he could feel its cold breath, breathing on him, but he knew he couldn't look at it.

"Daddy", it was his daughter's voice. "Daddy, please help me. I'm cold, Daddy."

The hermit kept his eyes closed. Cold, icy tears started to form in his eyes, and he could barely hold the tears under his eyelids as they filled up. It was a voice long gone; he knew it wasn't her, but it was the scarlet demon.

"Daddy, help me. It's so cold in here. Daddy, please. Don't let her take me to the well".

The hermit's eyes started to freeze, as they did when the black crow was being born, after the hunters killed that deer. She ran her hands down both sides of the chair and to his shoulders; he could feel the cold, lifeless touch of her hands.

"Daddy, please save. Save me".

He could take no more as his eyes couldn't hold back the freezing icy tears, and he stood up, "You took her away from me. She is gone."

The creature lifted its hands off his shoulder as the hermit slowly turned around to face the creature. "Daddy". A small child's hand tugged at his shirt. He opened his eyelids slowly in fear and looked down, It was his little girl. He slowly bent down as her warm hand touched his face; it felt just like it did all those years ago.

But was she really there? Could she be alive? But he buried her. "Oh my God," he said as his eyes started to focus; he could see more clearly. she looked as she did the night the creature took her. He wanted to wrap his arms around her, but the air started to become cold, and as his daughter breathed out, he could see the coldness of her breath in the air. "Daddy, why did you let her take me to the well?"

"What, well, baby? You are here with me".

Her voice deepened, losing its sweetness. "Daddy," she growled, "why did you let her take me to the well?"

"Her? Who's her, honey? Who is—" He paused, remembering the creature not as a woman, but something else entirely.

"Daddy, why did you bury me?" Her voice turned colder, heavier.

"Baby, I thought it took you from me. I… I didn't know…" Then he saw her skin pale and cracked like porcelain, like a broken doll. "Baby?"

"Daddy!" she roared, her voice thick with rage, her body beginning to fall apart. "Daddy!" she growled again, deeper, as the pieces shattered.

"No Baby, No!!!" As she fell to pieces in front of him, he was losing her again. She crumbled in front of him, and the pieces scattered upon the floor.

The hermit's head hung down as he cried and reached out to gather her pieces, but as he reached out, he could feel the feet of the creature as it took his breath away.

"You took her from me again, you bastard."

He stood up, knowing it was time to face the darkness that had taken his daughter. With his head still hung down, he took a deep, cold breath, filling his lungs with the cold air, and closed his eyes. As he looked up to face the darkness, he opened his eyes and saw it all in its dark glory, standing before him. The black crow cawed, but there were no eyes to gaze into, nothing but black holes where eyes should be. He stood in awe as he stared into the abyss of nothingness.

The creature grabbed his face, as he uttered the words "You bastard", he could only feel the cold as it frosted his face. The black crow cawed and flew to the creature's shoulder, gazing into the eyes of the hermit as he gazed back into its blood-red eyes. As he and the black crow stared into each other's eyes, his eyes began to bleed.

He could feel a pressure build in his eyes; they started to fill with nothing but red tears and pain. The creature started to grasp harder on his head and squeeze, the pressure was becoming unbearable inside his head and his eyes. As he began to speak, his brain started to succumb to the pressure, and the coldness intensified as his eyes bled more; the black crow cawed and stared into his eyes.

The hermit's eyes became blinded by the blood, but he could not speak or yell, but he could feel the pain, the pressure, the coldness. The black crow started to move its beak across the hermit's left eye, scraping its sharp tip across his cornea, scratching slowly, back and forth. Then to his right eye, as it continued going back and forth to each eye. Getting more and more furious and deeper and deeper as it passed the layers, though the iris's scraping down to the lens, and then it stopped.

The hermit could feel it all and couldn't scream as the pain became more unbearable; he could feel the blood running down his face. Then the black crow cawed as it jammed its beak deep into the hermit's vitreous chamber of his right eye, digging deeper and twisting and turning its head, digging deep till it started to reach his brain.

The black crow twisted and turned, as if searching for something, hunting for a thought. Then it moved to his left eye, repeating the same motion until it suddenly stopped. The hermit opened his mouth to scream, but no sound came. He tasted blood on his lips, warm and thick as it drained down.

He felt the crow's beak inside his skull, the unbearable pressure mounting. Slowly, the crow withdrew its beak. It raised its head and let out a piercing caw, blood, eye, and brain matter dangling from its beak.

The creature's grip tightened. The hermit felt himself slipping—drifting into the cold, consuming dark of death.

As the creature dropped the hermit's lifeless body to the ground, the black crow and the creature walked to the hermit's bedroom and shoved his bed over with a purpose. Then the creature bent down and threw the throw rug underneath the bed to the wall. The creature slid its open hand across the floor as it searched for something, and as it moved its hand back and forth, the black crow let out a screeching caw. The creature stopped its hand on one of the floorboards and laid it flat. The black crow cawed twice, and then the creature scraped its long nails across the floorboard, leaving deep scratches within the wood, splintering it. And then stopped to lift its hand into the air, its nails pointing down and with furious rage, brought it down through the floorboard, breaking it in two.

Below the floorboard was a chest locked with an old skeleton key, leather-handled straps, and wooden. The creature grabbed its leather old handles and pulled with one hard and furious upward thrust, breaking it out from the floor, breaking and splintering the floorboards around it. As the creature lay on the floor, it put its hands on each side of it, caressing it as if it were a lover. It started to freeze the chest with its cold touch. As the wooden chest turned to ice, the creature lifted its left hand into the air and brought it down with tremendous force, breaking it open and pulling out a black cloth cloak. It was what the hermit took from it so many years ago.

The creature stood up and admired it as someone does, looking at the newly bought dress, holding it out with both hands in front of it. The black crow cawed and flew off the creature's shoulder; the creature turned quickly around and draped the cloak over its head as it slowly pulled up its hood over its long, white hair. The black crow flew to the creature's shoulder and cawed as the creature slowly walked out of the hermit's bedroom, past his lifeless body. The black crow cawed, stopping the creature. The creature raised its hand above the hermit's daughter's porcelain remains, raising them into the air and consuming them into its body. And then continued out the door.

As Sandy stood in the room, still holding Leeann's cold hand, she wondered what had just happened. "Leeann, what just happened? How did you know everything was going to be alright?"

Leeann glanced over to the black and orange crow sitting still on the windowsill, gazing out into the gray landscape. "Sandy, let's get Frey settled down and I'll explain the best I can." Sandy, still confused, slowly let Leeann's cold hand slip from her as Leeann's hand started to turn warm again.

Sandy looked at Frey's eyes as Frey looked over to the windowsill, staring at the black and orange crow; it turned, looking back at Frey's eyes. As Sandy noticed that Frey's eyes started to close, as she dozed off into sleep. The black and orange crow then turned its attention back out into the grayness of the landscape as the wind picked up and the snow blew heavier and heavier across the sky. The sunlight was blocked by the heaviness of the gray clouds blanketing the sky with its haunting atmosphere. Sandy thought to herself, what was the black and orange crows' reason for being here? What was its connection to Frey? Was it a guardian or a threat? Sandy couldn't help but think that something was coming, and she didn't know what it was, but she felt uneasy.

As Leeann and Sandy prepared Thanksgiving dinner, Leeann started to explain, to the best of her ability, what had happened and how she knew it would be alright.

"As I looked into the crow's eyes, I felt fear. But the longer I stared, the calmer I felt. Even though what I saw would have frightened most, including me".

Sandy looked at her confused "What was it? What did you see?"

Leeann sighed, knowing what she was going to say was going to be hard to understand; she couldn't understand it herself. "Sandy, it felt so cold but warm inside. There was so much pain and death, so many bodies, rotting corpses, children stood frozen in time, but you could feel they wanted to scream, run, hide, cry, but they just couldn't. Then there was this well, this old brick gray well, and you could see creatures crawling out of it, snarling, drooling, and panting. They were crawling in and out, taking flesh into its depths. It looked like maggots layering the ground, but it was those creatures skimming through the flesh of the corpses that covered the ground."

Sandy studied Leeann closely. "But how did you know Frey would be alright? It sounds like a nightmare—terrifying. How in all that did you feel peace?"

"There was something out there," she said softly. "A figure in the distance—dark, but blurry. I couldn't make it out. Though the death, screams, and pain I could feel, there was a light above, something that told me that there was hope. This was a future we didn't have to live in; there was a way to stop it. I think Frey may be that key, that's why this crow", as she pointed at the windowsill, "is here. That's why it's keeping watch over her. I feel she is the key to ending this all. I just don't know how."

Sandy felt a strange mix of fear and peace, as if she understood something without fully grasping it. Deep down, she just knew—some things were good, some were evil, and there had to be a balance between them. And somehow, that balance was tied to Frey.

As Betty lay there in her white pajamas thinking about what was to come, she sat up at the edge of her bed and put her hands on her face. As she got up from her bed, she unplugged her cell phone, and walked into the living room, she then went into the kitchen to make a cup of coffee to wake up fully.

As the coffee brewed, she couldn't help but wonder when it would come for her and Nancy, but she now knew it was here; it had arrived. As she poured a cup of fresh coffee, she walked into the living/dining room and sat down. She took a sip of her coffee and glanced over to the snow globe on her fireplace mantle.

As Betty stared into the snow globe, it seemed to come alive. Snow began to fall gently within its glassy prison, delicate and slow. She knew this was the beginning—the moment she and Nancy had been warned about.

The snow thickened, swirling in quiet patterns. Then, it began to change. A gray fog began to fill within, like a heavy cloud of smoke, dancing within the globe. As the smoke filled the globe, the falling snow within started to turn black, like falling ash after a volcano erupts. She knew this was the 3rd and final sign of its coming, and it needed what Nancy and she had. As she looked down at her phone, she had laying on the table beside her cup of coffee, it went off. It was a notification from Betty.

Nancy: *Betty, the globe is changing.*

Betty picked up her cell phone.

Betty: *Yes, so is mine.*

Nancy: *You know what that means?*

Betty took a deep breath and typed back.

Betty: *Yes, the 3rd sign, it's coming for what we have.*

Nancy: *I'm on my way to you.*

Betty: *Ok, see you soon.*

As she laid her cell phone down on the table face down, she put both hands around her cup of coffee and raised it up for another sip and then looked out the window into the gray skies and blowing snow. She couldn't help but to think back to that faithful day that marked their long journey to this point and time. The day had come; their purpose has been fulfilled.

Betty and Nancy have been friends since the day they were born. Their mothers' had been friends since they were born, and down the line. The families have been friends for so long, through the family histories, that they might as well be blood. The same with their fathers. Their fathers' families have known each other since they can't remember when. It was like they all had a destiny. The mothers and fathers of both Betty and Nancy knew each other, so it was inevitable that they would end up together. Betty lived next door to Nancy, as the homes had been in their respective families for centuries.

On a wintry afternoon, Betty and Nancy, along with their mothers and fathers, did what they always did this time of year—set out together to find the family Christmas trees. But something about this particular year felt different. Maybe it was the timing, a little later than usual, or maybe it was the place they had chosen.

They gathered together into Nancy's family's old station wagon and went out to find the family Christmas trees. This year, they wanted to go out into the old barreling woods far out into the outskirts of town. As they parked the car and they all got out, with their fathers getting their axes out of the back hatch of the old family station wagon, Nancy and Betty both looked at each other " Do you hear that, Betty?"

"Yes, I do", Betty replied.

"What do you girls hear?" Betty's mother asked.

"Mommy, you don't hear the melody that you sing to us every night before bedtime?" Nancy's and Betty's mothers both listened for the melody.

"No girls. We don't hear anything but the crows cawing".

"Really, Mommy? It sounds like you". Nancy replied.

"Nothing at all". As Nancy's and Betty's mothers listened again.

"Maybe they are just being silly like they always are". Betty's mother told Nancy's mother as they smiled with a giggle. "Well, no mind, let's go, girls". Betty's mother said to Betty and Nancy.

They trudged through the snow, weaving between trees in search of the perfect Christmas tree. Betty and Nancy ran ahead, their laughter echoing through the quiet woods as they caught snowflakes on their tongues and pelted each other with playful snowballs.

The melody grew louder and louder as they ventured deeper into the woods. As the girls left their footprints behind scattered throughout the woods, their mothers and fathers looked around for the perfect trees for each of the respective houses.

"Hey, do you remember where we used to hunt, Homer?" Betty's father asked Nancy's father

"Oh yeah, Clarence, I remember. The pines just over that hill over there". He pointed in front of them. "I bet you we would find the perfect pines in there, it's deep and thick with a mile of pines". Homer said to Clarence.

"Yeah, let's look there". As they all started to make their way to the hedgerow.

"Look, Helen". Nancy's mother pointed at the trees in front of them.

"I see it, they're so beautiful, May", Betty's mother replied.

"Now girls, stay near, it gets thick as we get deeper in here". May said.

The girls giggled, and the melody got closer as they walked through the pines. "Homer, look at those two?" As Clarence pointed to the two trees in front of them after walking for 15 minutes into the pines

"Yeah, those two will work". Homer replied as May shouted out to the girls.

"Now go and play. Not too close to where your dads are cutting the trees down, but not too far".

"Yes, Mom". As they both continued to kick around the snow and tried to catch the snowflakes on their tongues.

As the girls played. Homer and Clarence pulled out the axe to start cutting down the trees one by one. Betty and Nancy could hear the melody coming from a clearing at the edge of the pines. The girls couldn't help but go and look, still giggling. The girls scurried around to the opening and peeked through the pines' thickness to see what was there.

The girls' eyes got wide as they saw a little old lady dressed in a black cloth hooded cloak sitting on the edge of an old foundation, humming the melody they heard from the minute they got out of the old station wagon. Betty and Nancy slowly crept out into the clearing, and the old woman stopped humming the melody, seeming startled.

"Who goes there?" She said in a raspy voice.

The girls stopped dead in their tracks. "It's just us", Betty replied.

"Who is *us*?" the old woman asked.

"I'm sorry if we startled you, ma'am. I'm Betty, and this is Nancy."

"What do you seek here, girls?"

Nancy looked confused.

"Oh, ma'am, our daddies and mommies are chopping down our Christmas trees in the pines over there", as she pointed into the pines.

The old woman giggled in a raspy voice, "What are you two doing so far away from your mommies and daddies then? The woods are dangerous. How old are you two?"

"We were told to say near but not too close as our daddies are cutting down the pines for Christmas by our mommies. We are 6 and 3 quarters old, ma'am". Nancy said.

The old woman snarled and giggled, "6 and 3-quarters old? Why are you girls here?"

"We heard your humming, your melody".

The old woman seemed surprised. "You both heard me humming?"

"Yes, we did, ma'am". The old woman seemed hesitant as she snarled, but knew she had to do what was to be done. After all, even so young, they heard the melody.

The old woman had hummed this melody for years, waiting for someone to hear. Only a few ever could hear her, and these girls were the first ones to hear for centuries.

"Well, listen closely and listen carefully, my little ones."

The girls were hesitant but not scared at all of the old woman's voice; the raspiness of it was as soothing as the melody she hummed. As the girls sat down in front of her, she reached into her old cloak and pulled out an old knife. As she slowly opened it, she reached into an old cloth bag and pulled out not one, not two, but three apples, handing one to each Betty and Nancy.

She used the knife to cut a sliver of an apple and brought it up to her mouth to take a bite. Her teeth were all black and rotting as she took a bite. The old woman grumbled as she chewed, the girls eating their apples as well.

"Now girls, did you know that you two are the only ones who have ever heard my melody?"

They both looked at the old woman and replied, "We are?"

"Yes, little ones, you are the only ones to hear my melody. That means you two were chosen to hear it. This means I will now have to fly away and be reborn as you take something I must give you".

"We are? We do?" the girls replied "Where are you going, ma'am?"

"Well, little ones, I have hummed that melody this time a year for many moons, many suns, and many, many years, forever it seems. Can I tell you girls a story before we part?"

"Yes, ma'am", they replied.

"Come here, little ones. I have a story to tell."

The girls moved closer and listened as they ate their apples.

The old woman cut another sliver off her apple and brought it up for another bite.

"My daddy owned this old foundation, the base of a home that once stood here long ago. He built it with his own two hands and claimed the rich land for crops to grow. But over time, the soil turned sour, and the crops wouldn't take. At which time, a man came knocking at our door, whom my daddy called the Dealer. This man offered to help replenish the dirt in the barren ground, but he had to place a key on our property to fertilize the land and bury it deep within the dirt below. This came with a price that would save the land, but take my daddy's life way too soon. The Dealer would collect, but I would have to be cursed to this land, waiting for someone to hear my melody. So, for centuries, I've waited for someone to hear, and through those times, I slowly began to lose all hope. That I'd lose the curse and be able to fly away"

The old woman began to seem more hesitant, as if it was becoming harder for her to speak. The girls seemed more intrigued.

"What happened next, ma'am?"

The old woman became more reluctant, but she had to keep going. She knew her time was limited in this form and she had to tell them as much as she could, but she felt the time starting to get shorter.

The old woman knew that for every bite the girls took was like an hourglass, and she knew that when they got down to the core, she would have to fly away.

"Slow down, little ones. You don't want to choke on the apples."

"But ma'am, they are so good". Betty said

"Yeah, so good, ma'am", Nancy replied.

"Well, little ones, time is of the essence."

As she put down her apple and the knife she had used to cut the slivers off, she reached into her ragged old bag, from which she pulled out not one but two globes. The girl's eyes looked in anticipation and delight. "Now, little ones, I must warn you that these globes have secrets within. As time will reveal, upon closer examination, you will gain a deeper understanding. Remember, when evil comes, it will show you, as good arrives to conquer evil, you will know. Good can see both good and evil, and pure evil can only see evil; it sees nothing more, being blind to goodness. So, you will know its power of evil, but you will see; only you two will see its weakness. Evil will come someday to collect these globes".

As the old woman's voice became raspier and cracked more with every fading breath she took. She knew time was close as the girls ate the apples to the core. "You will have to sacrifice much, but you will save more. Never lose sight of good and always beware of evil, and you will see everything clearly".

The girls nodded their heads as they seemed to understand, staring into the two globes, eating down to the core. The old woman handed them the globes and said as her voice faded.

"Run along, little ones. Remember the key to it all will be born and the key is…" as the old woman's voice became silent as she could no longer speak.

The girls threw their cores on the foundation floor, and they walked away. The old woman faded away, and all that was left was her old cloak. The core of the apples slowly sank into the foundation floor. The girls could hear their mothers "Betty, Nancy, where are you? Betty, Nancy". The girls with their globes in hand started walking back to their parents.

"Over here, Mom". As they made it back into the pines, following their mother's voices.

"Where were you two?" Nancy's mom asked.

"Look, Mom. Look what we found," Betty said.

"Where did you two get…?"

Betty woke up out of her daydream when she heard the knocking at the door of her place.

As Betty got up to open the door, she could see the globe rain heavier with the black soot from the corner of her eye. She knew that the end of the road was here and she knew Nancy was standing on the other side of the door. As she opened it up, Nancy, holding her globe covered with a towel

"Hey Betty, is dinner ready?"

Betty grinded "No, I was waiting on you"

"Well, let's get to cooking. Tonight is going to be a long night, A night we have been waiting for, for so long".

As they whipped up something simple for their Thanksgiving dinner, they joked and reminisced about the days of growing up laughing about the years after they got the globes.

As Nancy and Betty sat down to eat, Nancy looked at Betty.

"Do you ever regret not having a family of your own?"

Betty let out a sigh, "Yes, but at the same time no".

Nancy looked at her and said, "Me too, I wish I did have a family, a husband, and kids."

Betty watched her across the table.

"But we didn't know what we would have carried onto them. Nancy, I have to tell you something."

"What is it?" Nancy asked.

Betty sighed and teared up a bit and looked down for a moment, as Nancy put her hand on Betty's back and rubbed it.

"What is it, Betty? Are you scared? I am too honey."

Betty teared up more and shook her head.

"No, it's not that. Remember the old hermit from the woods out beyond the pines?"

"You mean Lukas?"

"Yes" Betty replied.

"Yes, that was a long 2 years that we didn't see each other. But we spoke when you two moved to Ethel Lake, but you both came back, and it was hard after the breakup."

"Well, there was more to that story. Much more."

As Betty told Nancy that after they moved, she and Lukas started to become sick, which is why she never sold the house here. But during that time, just before they moved to Ethel Lake, Betty became pregnant and she knew she didn't want to abort the baby. She wanted to keep the child, but she knew that it would carry her curse.

Betty explained, "This is why I gave you the globe and we left. After the baby was born, I started to have a mystery sickness, and things went downhill with the relationship from there."

She said she left, leaving Lukas a note not to follow. Nancy was shocked—she had no idea. But she had her own dark secrets.


Betty went on. Lukas had come back, but she didn't know until two years later. She stayed away, afraid the baby would inherit her curse. She'd heard he was living beyond the pines, but they both kept their distance.


Betty began to sob as she said the last part.

"Remember the winter that the children of the town disappeared?"

"Yes, Betty".

"Well, that was what is coming for us."

"I know, Betty". Betty sobbed more and it became harder for Nancy to understand her.

"What? What are you trying to say, Betty? Wait, I remember, he lost, oh my God! Wait. That was your daughter?"

"Yes." Betty tried to say as she sobbed uncontrollably.

As Nancy rubbed Betty's back and reached for a tissue, she whispered, "It's alright." Then, after a pause, she added, "Betty... I have something to tell you."

As Betty collected herself, Nancy began to tell her story. She began to tell Betty about the same time when Betty and Lukas left town all those years ago. When they left, Nancy had met Jack, an auto mechanic who owned the old shop down on Old Townline Road, and about how they fell in love after her car broke down in front of his shop. As the months progressed, she became pregnant with twins. She didn't have the heart to abort them, just as Betty didn't have the heart to abort her daughter.

"During childbirth, the baby boy didn't make it—complications no one saw coming. But the girl survived. We named her Leona. Still, I knew she couldn't stay with me. I explained to Jack and showed him the snow globe, and he thought I was crazy and didn't want me to be near Leona. As much as it hurt me, I knew I had to stay away from her, and he needed to get her out of town.

"Last I heard, he had moved near the town of Destiny after his shop burned down". Betty looked at her and thought for a minute,

"Wait, didn't that place burn down years and years ago?"

Nancy looked down, ashamed.

"I know. I needed him to take her far away, so I...I...I..."

Betty knew the answer to the question she had just asked Nancy.

Nancy looked at her and said, "I had no choice."

Betty looked at her and said, "I know. But what happened to her?"

"Last I knew, Jack had died of cancer and Leona was still alive in Destiny. But that was a long time ago".

Their confessions made them realize that they were stronger together now than ever. But the inevitable was the inevitable. They ate their dinner, quietly thinking.

Sandy and Leeann set the table for dinner as Fry lay sleeping on Leeann's bed, surrounded by pillows. The wind blew harder, rattling the windows throughout the house, and the snow intensified as it blew around more violently. As Sandy and Leeann sat down, with Leeann's back facing the window, where the black and orange crow was perched at the table. Sandy started to wonder, and fear set in. Could all that Leeann saw and heard be hallucinations? Was Leeann not who she seemed to be? But how did she know Frey would be alright? How did she *know*? So many things were left unanswered, and every person has their mysteries and unanswered questions. Every town has its secrets; its past, its tales, and its people have them as well. Sandy kept her thoughts to herself, but still the worry in the back of her mind of what Leeann was hiding and what was left unspoken.

Leeann felt something as she ate dinner with Sandy. She couldn't shake the urge to look behind her—at the orange-black crow on the windowsill. It was as if something was pulling her, demanding she turn. The feeling was undeniable. She set her fork and knife down and slowly turned to look.

The crow was still gazing out into the gray snowy lands in the distance. As the crow caught a fierce gust of wind, it started to shiver as it chilled the crow's bones. They could feel the fear and death that was coming for them in the air.

Frey started to whimper, lying on Leeann's bed. Leeann turned her attention to Frey and could see that Frey was starting to shiver, as the crow turned back to looking in the window, gazing at Frey. Leeann got up off her chair and walked to the bedside of Frey. She sat down next to her and reached down to touch Frey's face, it was cold, cold as ice. Leeann looked over to Sandy. Sandy could see something was wrong.

"What is wrong?" Sandy asked quickly.

"I don't know. She is so cold", Leeann mumbled.

Sandy set down her knife and fork and got up to go to Leeann and Frey's side. As she sat down next to Leeann, she could feel the coldness radiating off of Frey and could see her lips starting to turn blue.

"Feel her cheeks, they're so cold."

Sandy started to place her hand on Frey's cheek; she could feel the cold through her fingertips.

"Oh my god, what is happening to her?" Sandy asked with deep concern in her eyes

"I don't know Sandy," as she pointed over to her throw blanket draped over the back of the couch. "Grab that blanket, let's try and get her warm".

Sandy got up with urgency and went over to the couch to grab the blanket. As she brought over the blanket to Leeann, Leeann was already covering her with what she had on the bed, swaddling Frey in it. Sandy gave Leeann the blanket from the couch and placed it around Frey's head. But nothing they did warmed Frey up, and she was radiating so much coldness, nothing they did helped.

Leeann and Sandy began to feel panicked as Frey grew colder and colder. Leeann felt this feeling and couldn't resist it; it was as if she was being called to look out the window at the orange-black crow. Leeann looked with fear and panic in her eyes, the crow gazed back at her, shivering as the snow started to cover its body, and Frey shivered more and more.

"What is it, Leeann? What's wrong?" Leeann slowly stood up off the bed.

"Leeann, what's wrong?" Leeann didn't answer; she couldn't take her eyes off the crow as it stared back at her.

"Leeann?" Sandy called out.

Leeann slowly put her hand out with her palm facing down and moved it up and down as she told her to keep it still with its movement. Sandy sat at the edge of the bed next to Frey, trying to keep her warm but also trying to keep her eye on Leeann.

Leeann walked slowly, step by step, across the room toward the windowsill as the crow and she kept their eyes locked on one another. As she crept closer to the windowsill, a cold chill filled her body, right through her warm flannel pajamas. The closer she got, the more she felt the coldness in her bones; she could feel what Frey and the crow felt. The bitterness, the chill. As she got to the windowsill, she stopped and slowly began to bend down. The air became cold as she took a deep breath, and the room grew dimmer with darkness.

Not taking her eyes off the crow's eyes, she continued her descent to the crow's level and stared deeper into its eyes. As she and the crow became face to face with only a thin layer of old glass between them, she felt all she had felt before when Frey had her seizure, all the fear, wonder, death, peace, and darkness. The crow shivered, and Frey shivered as the coldness became more intense. Leeann exhaled the air she held in her lungs, and she could see her breath.

Sandy felt fear but kept watching as Leeann and the crow looked at each other. Leeann began to raise her left hand to the latch on the window, as it was locked, covered in white paint for years due to its non-use and subsequent painting over. As she gripped it, she started to turn it.

"Leeann—" Sandy whispered.

As Leeann started to break through the old paint and move the latch, the crow looked up at the latch and then back into Leeann's eyes. Leeann never took her eyes off the crow. As the latch became fully unlocked, she moved her left hand back down with caution, and the crow followed its movement. Leeann looked at the crow as it locked eyes with her again. She reached up again with her left hand and slid it up the window, the crow's eyes followed. As she did, the window started to open as it broke through the paint more and more.

"Leeann?" Sandy started again.

She still kept her eyes on the crow as the window slowly cracked open. The crow looked back into Leeann's eyes as the window opened just enough for the crow to come in. The wind and snow blew into the house as Sandy moved in close to Frey, snuggling with her, trying to keep her warm and shield her from the cold that came from the open window. Leeann brought her hand back down, her and the crow staring at each other with nothing between them.

Leeann raised her right hand to the windowsill, palm up and open. The crow cawed once, then lifted its left foot to rest in her palm, followed by its right. Sandy took a deep breath, holding it as the cold air filled the room.

Leeann slowly stood, closing the window with her free hand and bringing the crow close to her face. They locked eyes—an intense stare that washed away Leeann's fear.

The crow stepped from her palm onto her shoulder. Leeann turned left, then spun to face the bed, and began walking back toward Sandy and Frey.

As Leeann carried the crow towards the bed, it then stopped shivering, and the room started to become warmer and warmer with every step. Sandy could feel that Frey was warming up and looked at Leeann with amazement in her eyes. She couldn't understand how, but she knew there was some kind of connection between Frey and the crow.

Leeann and the crow got to the bedside, and Leeann sat down on the bed next to Frey. She raised her right hand up to her shoulder, the crow stepped into the palm of her hand, and Leeann brought it to her face again. Leeann and the crow gazed at one another for a second as Leeann and the crow seemed to understand one another.

"Please, please, be what I hope you are."

As she brought her hand down to the bed, the crow looked at Frey and tilted its head back and forth, left to right, as it looked at Frey sleeping on the bed. They were both warm to the touch as Leeann felt the warmth of the crow and Sandy felt the warmth of Frey.

The crow stepped off her hand and started to move toward Frey, walking to the front of her. It brought its beak down, moving the covers around Frey, like it was tucking her in for a nap. The crow pulled some of the covers down with its beak and snuggled into Frey's chest and looked at Leeann. Leeann, almost like she knew what it wanted, covered the crow with the blanket. Sandy looked at this all as it was happening and then looked at Leeann.

"What is happening here? What does this mean?" She whispered.

"I don't know, but there is a connection". Whispering, as they sat there staring at the crow and Frey. The crow gazed out of the window as Frey slept.

Betty and Nancy finished their dinner and began to clear the table as the snow globes continued to fill up with the black soot snow. Nancy couldn't help but wonder how Betty knew about the orange and black crow.

"Betty, how did you know that night in the hospital?"

Betty looked at Nancy.

"Remember that day we got the globes?"

Nancy nodded her head.

"The day we got them, I was in my bedroom and I put the snow globe on my dresser and ran out of my room to have dinner. Mom was calling for me, asking if it was ready. When we were done eating, I think it was Mac and Cheese, Mom said it was time for bed. I went up, brushed my teeth, and put on my *My Little Pony* PJs and got snuggled into my bed. Mom came in, tucked me in, and kissed me goodnight. As I dozed off, I gazed at the glow emanating from the snow globe and drifted off into sleep. As I fell deeper into sleep, I began to see images of a black, red-eyed crow, and I started to feel fear; I knew this was the evil crow. But as the night progressed, I began to see something in the distance, and it was blurry at first. It came more into focus, and it was a black and orange crow. The same one that sat on that windowsill that night when the girl gave birth to the baby. I felt a sense of peace within that crowd that day in the hospital, and somehow I knew it was the image I had seen all those years ago. It was indeed that crow, that's how I knew. But if you're asking me that, how did you know what I was talking about?"

Nancy looked at Betty as they washed the dishes.

"I don't know. I've seen so much since the nights after we got the snow globes from the old woman. Everything was a blur to me. I could make out different things, I could see shadows of color, but I knew that what you said felt right. The images that I couldn't see became vivid that day you told me about the baby and that woman in the hospital that day. There was something about that day that told me that the first sign was coming. I could feel it in the air, in the breeze, and there was something else that day that made me believe there was something."

Betty looked at her in a confused look.

"What was it?"

Nancy looked at her as they finished up the dishes, Nancy drying them. She leaned up against the sink counter, drying her hands with a dish towel.

"The night before you walked into that room, I could see it in your eyes, but I knew already. The night before was a new moon, and it was a harvest moon. I stayed up that night as I couldn't seem to sleep. As I gazed out through my bedroom window, the light of the new moon became orange and was peering through an opening in my curtains, it lit my room up. As I did, I heard a crow caw in the distance, and it made me realize that something was changing in the air, and I got an overwhelming feeling that something new was coming. The next morning, I was driving to work, and I couldn't shake the feeling that something was going to be different. And then it happened that night, and the ambulance arrived at the hospital, being the only one. As I heard over the loudspeaker that it was someone in labor, I somehow knew it was a sign; it was the only thing born that day. I knew that it was a sign that something was coming, and I knew with one that something else was coming. I felt our destinies were upon us."

As Betty and Nancy finished the dishes, and the gray of the sky became darker as night fell upon the town of Garville, they both waited for it to come. The snow globes were almost full of nothing but that black soot. Betty and Nancy mentally prepared for the inevitable. As the snow globes filled to the top, they waited and waited for it.

Betty started to feel the coldness settle in, and so did Nancy. The wind picked up, and the snow became blinding out the window. As the wind gusted and the snow became blinding, the darkness became blacker than black. Nancy looked over at Betty, feeling the chill of the cold rush down her spine

"It's almost here". She muttered.

"I know Nancy, I know".

They both heard the windows rattle, startling them both as they continued to look at each other with fear. Then they heard a scratching at the window, just in the living room from which they sat. Nancy looked and could see red eyes peering in at them through the curtain. Betty didn't look back, but could see it on Nancy's face as she was looking at the window.

"Betty, it's here". She barely whispered.

The room became colder and colder; they could both see their breath as they exhaled. The room started to freeze as the glasses still left on the kitchen counter started to form frozen cracks, then they shattered, popping like a balloon that had been overfilled with air, which startled them both.

As they turned to look at the glasses, they were overcome with a sense of dread. Their lips began to turn blue. Glancing back at each other, they gasped—only to freeze mid-breath. Their lungs locked, their limbs paralyzed, and even their eyes refused to blink. The room began to glaze over with ice.

They could hear every sound but couldn't scream. Then, from a distance, they heard a pecking sound. It grew louder and louder. It sounded like a beak hitting against the ice that started to crack.

As they sat there unable to move, breathe, speak, or scream, a black crow landed in-between them on the table and lifted its head and cawed loudly as if it was calling something. As they sat there looking with their frozen eyes, the fear began to take shape in their heads.

The black crow hopped over to Nancy and then gazed into her eyes, tilting its head side to side; its beak mere inches from her left eye. Nancy couldn't do anything but stare helplessly. Then it moved to her lips, tugging at them with its beak, as blood welled from the cracks, split open by the bitter, freezing air.

As the bird pulled on them, the blood began to trickle out and onto it's beak. The crow began to rip off the skin of her lip, layer by layer, and it began pulling harder and harder. It peeled the layers from left to right, then back again—ripping and scraping—until her lips were nothing but shredded meat, blood dripping steadily onto the table below.

The black crow then turned its attention to Betty. Hopping across the table with bits of Nancy's lips still dangling off it's beak. Betty sat frozen in fear, unable to stop it. As it got to Betty's face, it stared into her eyes and looked deep into her. She could feel it in her head as it was searching for something.

Every side-to-side movement it made with its head, tilting back and forth, Betty could feel it digging around in her brain. As it stopped, it started to nibble at her left eyelid. Peeling at it as it cracked and bled, pulling at it like it was rubber. The crow kept ripping at it, and then it did the same to the right eye. Shaking its head as it tore into her cold flesh, filling her eyes with blood. She could feel all the pain, all the tears, in her frozen flesh.

As the crow tore her eyelids away, letting them dangle from its beak before her exposed eyes, it threw its head back and cawed into the sky. Then it strutted to the center of the table, its cries growing louder and more frenzied with each shriek.

The door to the house behind Nancy started to freeze and crack through, then a hand burst through it. Black and cold as death, steam radiated off of it. Then, with a thunderous crash, it burst through the door—splintering it like glass to the floor—finally revealing its true form.

With its black, ragged cloak torn and tattered hanging off of it, it slowly walked to the table with its head held down. It turned to face the table, where the black crow stood motionless, blood and torn flesh dripping from its beak.

The crow stopped cawing as the creature looked up, displaying her female face and two black sockets where her eyes belonged. As it took in a cold, snarling, deep breath, it began to raise its hands to the mantle above the fireplace and pointed to the snow globe filled to the rim with blackness.

The crow cawed as it flew off and landed on top of the snow globe, grabbing it from the stand on which it stood. As the creature turned its hand palm up and extended all its fingers out, the black crow placed it in the creature's hand. The creature took its other hand and rubbed the snow globe, as if it were rubbing a pregnant belly, and then squeezed it into its hands, shattering the glass surrounding it.

It put it's one hand down as it held the black inside of the snow globe in its hand. It grinned as it raised the globe to its empty eye socket. It shoved the globe into the cavity, adjusting it until it sat comfortably.

As the creature brought its hand down, the eye began to move up and down, side to side as it walked over to the mantle, to get the other one and shatter it and insert it into the other empty eye socket. As it stood there, facing the mantle, it turned its attention back to Betty and Nancy sitting at the table. It snickered and groaned as it walked back to the table.

Betty could only watch as it stopped behind Nancy and placed its hands on her shoulders as it did to the hermit. Nancy could feel a chill emanating from it's hand. But then it glanced at Betty and walked to her. This time, Nancy watched as it did the same to Betty. Immediately, Betty felt it. The death of the man she loved, and her only child. Betty felt every morsel of pain that her child felt as she lay dying her father's arms.

*"I'm so cold, daddy. So cold,"* she could hear her daughter's voice echo.

The creature made her feel the pain and hear her daughter's voice as the creature bent down and sniffed her fear, her pain, her hurt, her cold flesh. As the creature stood up, it moved its hands to each side of Betty's face. Nancy could see its nails extend on both hands and sink into Betty's cheeks. Blood started pouring down the sides of her face. As the coldness of the air took hold, the blood and flesh began to stiffen and freeze. The creature licked off the blood from its fingertips.

The creature then started to walk over to Nancy. Nancy knew she was next and knew she was about to face the creature's wrath.

As the creature licked more of the blood from its hands, it took it's place behind Nancy. As it placed its hands on her shoulders, it bent down, as it did with Betty and it smelled her fear. Then it licked her cold flesh, Nancy could do nothing as it snarled. It ran its hand down from the top of Nancy's face, smearing Betty's blood and flesh down her frozen skin. As it ran back up her face, it stopped with its sharp nails at Nancy's eyes and started to dig its sharp nails into her eye sockets, slowly puncturing into her eyeballs and her brain, twisting its fingers as it searched for something.

As if reading her thoughts, her pain, and her past, her present. As it moved around her brain, it found what it was looking for. What it wanted, but why it wanted it was unclear. Nancy could feel it scratch and claw for her memories, and as it did, it stopped. It seemed to have felt something, Nancy tried not to think. But she had no choice but to think of her past, the child she had, the man she had it with, and then she saw it. She could see that her daughter alive and well. She also saw that the creature knew what had happened to her as she walked out into the snow that night.

*"Ah, Mommy, it's you…"*

As Nancy drifted off into the darkness of death, she could hear the echoes of what it spoke to her.

As the creature pulled its fingers from Nancy's eyes, it licked its fingers as the flesh and blood ran down. The black crow flew up to the creature's shoulders and cawed. As Nancy and Betty's bodies began to defrost and slump over the table, the creature walked out into the wind and snow, then off into the night.

Leeann and Sandy watched as the black and orange crow lay snuggled up with Frey. Frey slept as the crow kept its eyes peering out the window as the snow and wind picked up. As Leeann and Sandy started to clear the table, Sandy looked at Frey and the crow.

"Leeann, what do you think the connection is? What do you think the crow is protecting her from?", Sandy inquired.

"I don't know Sandy. I know that there is something coming, but I don't know what", Leeann said, glancing at her baby with the crow.

Sandy looked at Leeann with a puzzled expression.

"How do you know it's protecting her from something?"

"I don't know, I just do," Leean shrugged. "I can tell when I gaze into the crow's eyes, I can feel it. I just know, and it has something to do with that dark, cloaked figure I saw in the flashes it gave me. I don't understand it, I may never understand it".

Sandy took a deep breath. "You don't think that Frey is some kind of sacrifice, do you?"

Leeann looked at Frey and the crow, then back at Sandy, and hung her head. "I don't know. I just don't know."

As the day faded into blackness, the wind and snow intensified. The black and orange crow stood watch as Sandy and Leeann did the dishes and cleaned up for the night. Frey and the crow stayed snuggled together.

"Do you need me to stay here with you tonight, Leeann?"

"No, Sandy, it's okay. Get home and I'll see you in the morning", Leeann smiled tiredly at her friend.

Sandy was hesitant to leave them alone after the night they all had. "Are you sure? It is no problem; I would just have to grab a few things from the house."

"I'm sure, we should be fine. But thank you", said Leeann, reaching out to squeeze Sandy's hand.

Sandy grabbed her jacket from the coat rack, put it on, got her boots on, and opened the door. She turned back around once more to face Leeann.

"Honey, I'm only a text away if there is anything you need."

Leeann smiled, and they both gave each other a hug.

"Thank you, Sandy. Thank you."

They both said they loved one another, and Sandy walked away as Leeann closed and locked the door.

Leeann turned the lights off and went to lie down on the couch, seeing as Frey and the crow had the bed. She kept watching over the two as she started to doze off. Her mind raced, pondering the connection between them and this strange bird. What was its full purpose, and what did it want with Frey?

Leeann lay sleeping on the couch as the crow gazed out the window for hours, guarding Frey. Then Leeann felt this pain, a pain like never before in her eyes. She reached up and covered them with the palm of her hands, rubbing them and tossing and turning, trying to get comfortable. The crow took notice as the wind picked up and rattled the windows through the house; the crow stared at Leeann as Leeann started to groan in pain. Leeann could feel something digging deep into her eyes, moving like fingers in her eye sockets and in her head. The crow wiggled out from the covers, careful not to wake Frey, and it took flight to the arm of the couch at

Leeann's feet and watched as Leeann twitched and turned with her mouth open, but no scream came out. Leeann could feel the pressure as it dug deeper into her head, twitching and scratching.

Frey's eyes opened wide; the black and orange crow turned to Frey and let out a coo. Frey's eyes did not blink; she just stared out into what seemed like nothing, gazing into the world. Frey started to breathe faster and faster, like she was hyperventilating, her heart racing, pounding out of her chest.

Then everything stopped. Frey's heart stopped. Her breathing stopped. Her tiny body lay lifeless, her eyes wide open, and her lips blue.

Leeann was still tossing and turning, trying to stop the pain digging into her head. The crow cawed in pain, then Frey's eyes started to seep blood, slow tears of blood started to run down her face as she lay there, lifeless. As Leeann felt the pain and the scratching and twitching inside her head intensify. The blood coming from Frey's eyes started to flow faster and faster, filling her eyes more and more with blood as it streamed down her cheeks, down her face over her blue lips, and into her mouth.

Leeann heard a voice; it sounded so familiar, but it was different. It had a rage-filled tone and was raspy, yet it was familiar.

"There you are, mommy."

Leeann sat up, screaming and covering her eyes still. The crow cawed, and Leeann dropped her hands down and turned her head quickly to Frey. She could see the blood on her face, and it was pooling in her eyes.

"Oh god!" Leeann gasped.

As she sprang off the couch and over the back of it to Frey's bedside.

Crying, she continued to shriek, "Frey? Frey!"

She grabbed Frey from under the covers. Holding Frey's head on her shoulder as the blood ran down the back of her shoulder, she looked at the crow as it cawed and cawed.

"Help her! Please, do something!" she screamed at the crow.

She panicked and paced around the room looking for her phone. Then she heard Frey sigh deeply and begin to cry. Leeann stopped pacing dead in her tracks; the crow stopped cawing.

Moving Frey in front of her, "Frey?" Frey stared at her crying, normal tears, washing down the blood from her eyes, cheeks, and face. Leeann, still in tears, put her back on her shoulder, holding her baby to her chest.

"Frey, my baby, Frey. What is happening to you?"

As Leeann and Frey began to calm down, Leeann changed her, made her a bottle, and laid her down on the bed and snuggled in with her. As Leeann lay there looking out the window holding Frey tightly, the orange black crow flew from the couch onto the pillows next to Leeann's head. "What do you want with her?" she whispered. "What is it that you need from her, us, why are you here?" Leeann looked into the crow's eyes to find answers, "Tell me, please, show me."

Leeann started deep into the crow's eyes and started to see fragments of answers…

The eyes began to tell the story as Leeann faded into the darkness of their stare. Leeann saw nothing but blackness and then opened her eyes. She was standing in a pumpkin patch as far as the eye could see, the trees were full and vibrant, the sun was almost too bright in the blue sky, and birds were chirping. Leeann stood there in the patch, looking at an almost perfect world full of beauty and hope. Leeann felt a light tugging at her pajama pants. The sun was so bright she had to readjust her eyes as she looked down to see what was tugging at her pajama bottoms. Her eyes began to focus, and she could start to make out a little girl staring up at her —a little blonde, curly-haired girl wearing a yellow sundress.

"Hello, honey."

The little girl grinned, staring up at her.

"Are you lost?"

The little girl shook her head no.

"Where are your mommy and daddy, honey?" The little girl giggled.

"Do you not understand me?"

The little girl nodded her head yes. Leeann started to crouch down to the little girl. As she crouched down as far as she could, she asked the little girl one more time.

"Honey, sweetheart, where are your mommy and daddy?"

The little girl giggled again and threw her arms around Leeann, holding her tightly in a hug. Leeann, surprised, took a second and put her hands around the little girl to hug her back.

"Oh, honey, thank you for the beautiful hug. But where are your mommy and daddy?"

The little girl whispered into Leeann's ear.

"Daddy is way out there…"

As she pointed into the distance, unwrapping one hand from Leeann's. She looked over to where the little girl was pointing, but the sun was too blinding, and she couldn't see anything. The little girl went back to wrapping her arms around Leeann.

"Honey, is your mommy nearby? I can't see your daddy."

The little girl started to sniffle, as if she were beginning to cry.

"It's ok, honey, what is wrong?"

The little girls sniffled more "My, my mommy… my mommy is not here I-,I- don't know if I have a mommy."

Leeann confused "Honey, it's okay, baby. But sweetie, how do you not know if you have a mommy?"

 The little girl sniffled more and more.

"I don't know if I do."

Leeann pulled the little girl from her embrace and put her in front of her, holding her arms between the elbow and the shoulder. The little girl wept with tears flowing down her face.

"Look at me, sweetie. Look at me, darling."

The little girl wiped her sniffling, runny nose with her arm and rubbing her eyes, looked at Leeann.

"Honey, you have a mommy. Everyone has a mommy, baby."

The little girl looked at her, still weeping a bit.

"But I don't, ma'am. I never remember my mommy".

The little girl then cheered up, her voice brightening, and she smiled.

"But I wish for her at the well and sometimes the well speaks to me in a woman's voice. Like it is my mommy, and she sings me lullabies, it's over there".

As she pointed down at the middle of the pumpkin patch, turning her head, Leeann looked at where the little girl was pointing, but again, the sun was just so bright, she couldn't see. She put her hand to her forehead as if she were trying to block the bright sun from her eyes. She turned back to the little girl.

"Honey, I can't see it."

The little girl is still pointing.

"It's over there."

Leeann still couldn't see anything, no matter how much she tried to block the sun with her hand; she squinted and still couldn't see anything. The little girl giggled, looked, and put her hand down to look at Leeann.

"Ha-ha. Here, ma'am."

The little girl put her hand out, palm up, as if offering to shake hands.

"Ha-ha, I'll show you."

Leeann looked at the little girl and smiled; she took her hand and stood up as they walked through the pumpkin patch towards where the little girl had pointed.

As they walked through the pumpkin patch, the little girl hummed a melody.

"*Hmmm hmmm, hmmm hmmm, hmmm hmmm hmmm*". As she started to skip through the pumpkin patch.

"Almost there." She said and continued humming the melody. Skipping and giggling away.

"Skip through the pumpkin patch, don't get your tootsies snatched…", she sang on.

Leeann smiled and giggled with her. When they reached the well, the little girl slowed down and looked up at Leeann. Leeann looked down at her. The little girl raised an index finger to her lips, "*shhh*," and then used the same finger to wave Leeann down.

Leeann bent down, whispering, "What?"

The little girl leaned into Leeann's ear.

"Now, we have to tiptoe up to the well quietly, ma'am. We don't want to wake them up," Leeann asked, confused. "Wake who up?"

"The people sleeping inside."

Leeann, still confused, played along.

"Ok, honey."

She slowly started to stand back up, and the little girl grabbed her arm and whispered.

"And ma'am, don't step on the pumpkins or the vines, please. That will wake them too."

Leeann looked down at the ripe, fresh pumpkins and the vines and whispered back, "Ok, honey, I'll follow you." As she stood up, she held the little girl's hand again as they tiptoed closer to the well.

As they got to the edge of the well, the little girl stopped and picked a flower from up in front of it. Leeann noticed it was a dandelion. The little girl let go of Leeann's hand and picked up petal after petal, throwing one after another in the well.

"Mommy, are you there? Mommy, I picked this just for you."

Leeann looked in wonder and listened intently for something from the well.

"What, Mommy? What did you say?"

The little girl whispered.

"No, mommy, she is my friend. I found her in the pumpkin patch".

Leeann couldn't hear anything but the little girl talking.

"Yes, Mommy, I think she is lost. I don't think she knows who she is, but she is really nice." The little girl turned around. "Ma'am, come closer, my mommy wants to meet you."

Leeann walked over, hesitant and slowly, to the edge of the well and looked in. She stared into the pitch-black abyss, not even able to tell how deep the well went.

"Mommy wants to know what your name is ma'am."

Leeann was confused and obliged.

"Hello, my name is Leeann."

Leeann could only hear her own voice echo down the well.

"Yes, mommy, I'm sorry."

Leeann could still hear nothing, but the little girl, standing behind Leeann as Leeann gazed into the well.

"Mommy asked me if I told you my name. I'm sorry I didn't."

Leeann smiled and was about to say something, but the girl continued.

"My name is Leona."

Leeann was in shock; her smile faded. "M-mom?" she stammered. When she turned around, she came face-to-face with her mother. Naked as she was the day she walked out into that blizzard. "Mom…how? Why— how are you here?" Tears welled in her eyes as she spoke, "I thought I lost you, mom."

Her mother stood there smiling at her.

"Leeann my sweet baby girl, look at you. You're all grown up, honey."

"Mom, how are you here right now?"

"Look baby, there is not a lot of time."

"But, Mom!"

A clap of thunder filled the sky, and clouds started to move in, darkening the sky.

"Mom, what is happening?"

Leona looked at Leeann.

"Honey, you have to be prepared for it to come."

The thunder grew louder and louder, drowning Leona's words. As lightning struck the trees, igniting them, splitting some right down the middle. The pumpkins started to rot below Leeann and Leona's feet. The dandelions withered, and the storm raged on. Leona kept speaking, but Leeann couldn't hear her.

"Mom, mom, I can't hear you".

Leona tried to speak louder and louder.

"Leeann, you and Frey will face…"

Voices started screaming from the well. The snarls started to become closer and closer, and Leeann looked back at the well, peering down it, she could hear creatures' nails clawing and scratch, and they tried to crawl out, getting closer and closer.

As the storm raged on, the creatures' snarls and screams from the well got louder. The thunder banged and banged, and lightning struck down. Leona's voice was more and more muffled, and then it all just stopped. Leeann slowly looked around from the well and saw the destruction. The trees burned, the sky blackened, the rotted pumpkins, and she felt the ground shift under her feet. It felt like slimy snakes moving over her feet. Leeann looked down and saw maggots all over her feet and legs; she could smell death in the air.

"Leeann!"

As she turned around, knowing it was her mom's voice, she saw it; it was the creature she had seen in the black, orange crow's eyes the first time they locked eyes, in a raggedy old cloak with its head hung down so you couldn't see its face. It slowly raised its arms into the air, and as it did, the ground began to shake, and the world around it became darker and darker. Lightning crawled above the clouds, lighting up the pitch-black night, and then it spoke to Leeann.

"Leeann!"

It brought its hands down quickly as the sky poured down blood, hitting the rotting pumpkins. As it hit the rotting pumpkins, hundreds of black crows flew from the rotten flesh of the pumpkins into the cold dark sky, cawing in unison as Leeann followed them with her eyes, "Leeann!!!' She slowly looked down at the creature before her. As she looked down to face it, it snarled at her, startling her, and she fell back into the well.

Leeann broke contact with the orange black crow's eyes and started to breathe hard, in cold sweats, as the crow looked back at her with sad eyes. Leeann knew that it was coming for her; she knew that it was coming for Frey, and she knew the crow was here to protect them.

Knock, knock, Leeann woke up.

"Leeann? Leeann, it's me, Sandy, honey."

"I'll be right there."

Leeann looked at the clock; it was early. 8:30 am, the clock read on her nightstand. Leeann got out of bed, trying not to wake Frey, and walked over to the door, unlocking it and letting Sandy in the door.

"Hey, honey. How was your night?" Sandy asked.

Leeann didn't want to say too much about what she saw last night.

"It went well," Leeann answered.

Sandy looked over at Frey and the crow.

"So, it went okay after I left?" Her voice was full of worry

With a worrisome tone to her voice. Leeann couldn't lie.

"A lot happened, but not to Frey. I just saw more that I have time to explain, but I will later".

Sandy nodded her head, and Leeann started making some coffee as Sandy closed the door and took her boots and jacket off.

"Let me get that for you, Leeann", Sandy said, reaching for the coffee.

"Go get yourself showered and dressed for work, I'll get the coffee brewing and change Frey."

"Are you sure?"

"Yes, I'm sure. Now get to getting honey, I got you covered".

"You are a lifesaver, Sandy".

Leeann gave Sandy a hug.

"I love you, Sandy".

"I love you too, Leeann."

And off Leeann went into the bathroom to get a shower. As Leeann started the shower and took off her pajamas, she reached her hand in to check if the water was getting warm. Old buildings always take time to warm up the water. As the water warmed and the steam filled the bathroom, Leeann got in the shower and let the warm water run down her body. She couldn't help but think of what she saw. What did her mother have to do with all this, and why did she disappear in the storm like she did that night, never to be seen again? As the water ran down her body to the drain, she couldn't help but think, What was in that well? Where was it, and what did it all mean? She had so many questions, but no answers.

After Leeann finished her shower, she turned off the water, dried off and wrapped her hair in a towel, and wrapped her body in another. She opened the door and saw the orange black crow sitting on the couch's arm and Sandy and Frey sitting on the bed. Frey looked at Leeann and cooed.

"Look, Frey, mommy's out of the shower."

Leeann walked over to Sandy and took Frey into her arms.

"My baby girl, how are you?"

Frey smiled and looked at her. Leeann smiled and held her in her arms, walking over to the coffee pot to pour a cup of hot coffee before getting dressed to go downstairs to work. As they sat down at the table, they began to talk.

"I love you, my bundle of joy."

Frey looked at her and yawned, and then smiled again at her. Leeann couldn't help but feel like she might lose her to whatever was coming, but Frey's smile showed her with a look in her eyes that she wasn't going to lose her. Sandy watched and could sense there was something, but she just poured her coffee and smiled as she leaned against the kitchen counter.

Leeann drank her coffee and stood up, and brought it to the sink. Sandy took Frey from her arms, and Leeann went to her dresser to grab some clothes, which she kept in the nursery. She closed the door behind her and got dressed in her blue jeans and red work shirt that read *Grady's Pizza Joint*. She opened the door and walked into the bathroom to brush her hair out and then put it up in a bun for work. As she came out of the bathroom, she saw Sandy and Frey sitting on the couch as Sandy was giving her a bottle.

The crow stood not far on the arm of the couch, watching every move that was made. Leeann knew that the crow was her guardian and nothing was going to harm Frey. The crow glanced at Leeann, Leeann smiled, and the crow looked right back at Frey. Leeann went over to Sandy and kissed Frey on the forehead.

"Mommy loves you, baby".

She then kissed Sandy on the cheek, "Thank you for everything."

Sandy smiled, "It's no problem, Leeann."

Leeann went to the door and put her shoes on, and said goodbye. As she opened the door, she couldn't help but glance back at Sandy, Frey, and the crow before shutting the door to go downstairs to work.

Leeann began preparing everything for the day. It was 10 am, and orders usually started coming in at 11 am. Leeann was getting everything washed up, the ovens heated, and made sure the place was up and running before old man Grady walked in the door.

Grady walked in at about 10 to 11 as the phone rang. He answered.

"Hello, Grady's Pizza." He paused and listened.

"Yep, I got it, 1 large pep and 30 wings. About 30 minutes," he paused again.

"No, thank you".

Grady looked at Leeann, "Well, looks like it's going to be one of those days, Lee."

Leeann smiled and started getting the dough, pepperoni, cheese, and sauce out as Grady got the wings going. The storm throughout the night calmed, and the snow was falling at a light, steady pace outside. Grady turned on some of his classic rock on the radio, listening to the morning team, Burt and Bruce, in the mornings on KPXT classic rock tracks.

As the stores in the area opened and the locals started walking up and down the sidewalks, the snow fell slowly, and everyone was doing their Black Friday shopping. The fire barrels were lit on the corners of each block so people could warm up. The town workers were prepping the streets for their Christmas decorations and the park on the corner, 2 blocks up on Main, were getting the lights untangled and unraveled for the big tree lighting for later tonight. The snow wasn't going to stop the town's big kick-off to the Christmas season.

As the calls came in at Grady's Pizza, the customers came in from the street, eating in and bringing shopping bags from the Main Street shops. Ordering slices, large pizzas, and wings for a bite to eat. As the day wore on and the orders kept the day going steady, the 2 hunters came in, Jack and Tom, still shaken up by what happened the morning before.

Jack and Tom walked up to the counter and ordered a large pepperoni, 10 wings mild, and two pops to go. As they waited for the pizza, wings, and pops they sat down at the counter

"Man, what was that yesterday?" Tom asked.

"Man. I don't know I haven't ever seen a fucking thing like it.", answered Jack.

"Dude, that shit was crazy," Tom said.

Jack still couldn't believe it

"We need to let it go".

Tom faced Jack "Man, I don't know how in the Hell a fucking bird can come out of that pumpkin, man"

"I don't know, man," Tom said with amazement.

Leeann overheard Jack and Tom's conversation; she couldn't help but think about what she saw as she stared into the black and orange crow's eyes. All those crows coming out of those pumpkins in the pumpkin patch shooting into the air like that, what did those hunters see? Leeann couldn't help but ask; she needed answers, she needed to know.

Leeann walked over to them, sitting at the counter.

"Excuse me."

The two men looked at her.

"I couldn't help but overhear your conversation".

"Oh, it's nothing—" Tom tried to brush it off.

"About the crow and the pumpkin," Leeann continued.

"Ma'am, I'm not sure what you mean," Jack joined in.

Leeann sighed, "Look, I know it sounds crazy, but I had a dream last night about crows flying out of rotting pumpkins and into the air."

Jack and Tom were taken aback and looked at one another. Tom looked back at her and waved her over, whispering so no one could hear.

"You mean you have seen this before?"

"Well, what did you see? What happened?" She asked.

Jack turned to Leeann.

"Well, ma'am, we went out to the woods just before dawn and sat way up in the woods. We had a trail cam set up, and we were hoping this buck we had seen since the beginning of the season would show up."

Leeann looked at Jack as if to continue.

"Well, ma'am, we used this old pumpkin from the back of the truck as bait, we didn't have any apples or corn. We set it up next to this old maple tree and waited, as the sun was about to break the buck showed up and I took the shot, that buck went down."

Leeann looked at them and whispered.

"What happened next?"

Jack looked at her with eyes that looked frightened. In fact, he was too scared to say anything.

"It was strange; the blood splattered on the pumpkin and this old man walked up freaking the fuck out. The wind and snow began to come down like mad."

Tom took a deep breath and continued where Jack left off.

"Well, the man screamed and yelled but the wind was blowing, y'know, and that pumpkin began to pulsate and glow, it was fucked ma'am."

Jack then looked at Tom and continued.

"Then this crow just crawled out of it, breaking though the damn thing, it was insane. Like who knew a pumpkin could do that, we thought crows came from eggs or shit like that."

Leeann looked surprised by that comment, but again was still interested by what they had to say.

"What happened then?" She asked.

"The old man was so upset, we thought he was pissed we shot the buck but then we thought maybe he knew what was happening. But that crow flew off into the sky."

Tom chimed in.

"Ma'am we got our deer and said fuck this and dragged that shit to our truck. We knew something was wrong; we got our asses up out of there. Pumpkins birthing a crow? Ma'am I looked that shit up on that Google thing, yeah that don't happen."

Leeann looked at them like *really*? They really thought that pumpkins gave birth to crows, but she thought the worst part is they had to look it up. All she could do was look at them and say: "Yeah, ok, thank you, your order will be up in a few."

She turned around and raised her eyebrows in the air, and mouthed the words *Holy shit.*

As she walked away to get the pizza out of the oven.

Sandy still couldn't believe all she had seen the night before. She couldn't understand what the orange crow wanted with Frey and Leeann. But Sandy had heard a story from years ago that had been passed down from generations before of this land. She remembered something her mother had said that she was told, and her mother's mother told her, and further down the family line. There where old stories about the town and the towns that surrounded this one, that the land was spoiled and that the lands and towns beyond the town of Garville had their own stories of ancient creatures that roam each town. How these creatures all had their own stories of things that happened, and the land in the middle of all this, a place that each child was told never to enter because of the evil within it.  That there was a place where evil lay and that only 1 chosen from each town could enter it, and each town had waited for the "Chosen Ones" to lift the curses. But she believed they were just stories, ancient myths that parents told their children to keep them in line and scare them, old campfire stories handed down by town's people.

As the day became later and later, the snow outside became heavier and heavier. The lighting of the town's Christmas lights and Main Street would have to wait till tomorrow night. The mayor, Mark Bliss, had places shut down early so people could get home before the snow was too bad, so bad that people couldn't see. Grady and Leeann started cleaning up the shop after closing at 5 pm, when the mayor's order took effect for the night. No cars or people were to be on the streets after 6 pm. Get home, stay warm, and buckle down, everyone was told.

Leeann looked at Grady and said, "Hey, I got this; you need to get home before you can't."

"Ah. Leeann, after living here for years and growing up here, this is just another storm."

Leeann smiled, "Maybe, but I'll clean up, you get home and keep warm, I've got this."

Grady smiled and got his jacket and as he put it on.

"Fine, fine, Miss Leeann, I'm going, I'm going, and you sound like my wife."

Leeann laughed and smiled "Yeah, yeah, well, she sounds like a smart woman, and she has to put up with your old crotchety ass, right?"

Grady grumbled and smiled, "Ya, ya, just don't forget to lock up and turn off the lights, goodnight honey," and opened the door.

"Night, Mr. Grady, I got it."

Leeann said as she threw a towel over her shoulder. Grady waved his hand and closed the door.

Leeann cleaned up and did the dishes as she looked out the window here and there. One minute, she could see Johnson's Liquor store, and the next glance out the window, she could barely make it out. The snow was coming down slowly but heavily, and then it got heavier.

Soon she could see nothing as it piled up on the sidewalk and the street. She had seen and heard the plow come up the street periodically, but soon she couldn't even see the orange lights on it, blinking on and off. She mopped the floors, emptied the trash, and wiped down the counters before calling it a night. By the time she was done, it was already 7:15 pm and it was time to lock the doors and turn off the power. She grabbed some left-over pizza for her and Sandy and opened the door to go upstairs.

As Leeann went up the steps to her apartment, she started to feel that something was not right. The wind started to blow, and she knew there was no way Sandy was leaving tonight. She opened up the door to her apartment and saw the black and orange crow sitting on the windowsill inside, looking out the window. Sandy was sitting on the couch and holding Frey in her arms. Frey was looking around as Leeann set the pizza down on the counter she had brought up from downstairs. She walked over to them. Sandy looked at Frey.

"Mommy's home, little one, look."

Frey smiled a little bit as Leeann walked over to her and looked down at her.

"Hey, baby girl."

"Do you want her?" Sandy asked.

"Let me get this stuff off and into my pajamas."

Sandy sat with Frey as Leeann went to the bathroom and cleaned up a bit. Leeann looked into the mirror after washing her hands and her face. The water dripped off her face. She started to look deeper into the mirror. She looked down for a second to splash some water on her face and then looked back at the mirror. As she did, she saw her mother's face staring back at her. She was startled and rubbed her eyes, then looked again; it was her mother's face staring back at her.

"Mom?" she whispered.

"Beware!"

Her mother's reflection warned. She rubbed her eyes again and looked again, and standing behind her was the creature in the black cloak. Leeann turned around, startled to look behind her, and there was nothing. She looked back into the mirror and was startled again as she saw the black crow staring back at her. Leeann startled and took a step back, and stumbled into the wall behind her.

"What the…?" She rubbed her eyes and looked again, but nothing but her reflection stared back at her. She grabbed the towel hanging on the rack next to the sink and dried her face off. She put it back on the rack, opened the door, and went to change in her pajamas.

She walked out in her flannel pajama bottoms and her white tank top. "Well, Sandy."

Leeann said, "Guess it's a slumber party tonight."

Sandy looked at her and then out the window.

"Damn, yeah I guess it is."

The snow was so blinding outside the window that Sandy knew she was going to be staying the night.

"But I have no clothes."

Leeann looked at Sandy.

"I got you covered," Leeann replied and walked over and grabbed Sandy some pajamas

"Here you go. These should fit just right". She handed them to her, taking Frey, and held her in her arms. Sandy went into the bathroom to change into the black pajama pants and the white shirt Leeann had handed her. As she changed, she thought about telling Leeann what she had remembered of the old town's stories, but after the long few days and everything, she decided not to burden Leeann with any more things.

After changing and coming out of the bathroom, Sandy saw Leeann changing Frey and getting her ready for bed in her flannel pajamas. Leeann looked at Sandy after changing Frey.

"Do they fit?"

Sandy nodded her head. "Yes, I guess they do."

Leeann had already made up the couch for Sandy for the night.

Leeann got Frey settled down and put some pillows around her.

"Well, let's get something to eat."

She grabbed the pizza she brought up and laid it on the counter. They both sat at the kitchen table and ate their pizza.

"We might have a tough night ahead of us."

Leeann looked at the crow looking out the window.

"Yeah, maybe."

The wind rattled the windows, and the snow was dense; it had become all that could be seen. The windowsill was covered in snow; the crow looked back at Leeann and Sandy. Leeann got up off her chair and walked over to the crow with a piece of pepperoni; the crow took it gently out of her hand and ate it. Leeann looked back over to Sandy after taking a look out the window.

"Sandy, I feel like it's going to be a long night."

"Why?"

Leeann looked back out of the window.

"I don't know, I just do," as she turned around and looked at Frey.

"I just do."

Leeann walked back over to the kitchen table and sat down, rubbing her face with her hands.

"Everything alright, Leeann?"

"Yeah, yeah, just beat."

"Well, let's get to sleep," Sandy said.

"Ya, we should", as they both lay down.

"Night, Leeann."

"Night, Sandy," as she turned off the lamp on her nightstand.

The storm outside was blinding; 10 inches fell every hour, and the plows couldn't keep up with the snowfall. By the time midnight rolled around, the town was paralyzed; no one was getting in, and no one was getting out.

The black and orange crow stared out of the window as if it were a guard. Leeann, Frey, and Sandy slept. But the crow noticed Leeann was not sleeping soundly, she would mumble in her sleep, which caught the crow's attention. The crow looked at Leeann and Frey. It could be seen that Leeann was dreaming of something as she muttered in her sleep.

Leeann walked through the darkness of the rotting pumpkins in the pumpkin patch in the pajamas she had fallen asleep in. She could feel the slimy ground, as she was not wearing any shoes or socks, but she could see what she was stepping on. Black crows flew above her as the clouds were black and streaks of lightning filled them, lighting up the sky. The black ash fell like snow, hitting the ground and being almost absorbed by the ground below. As she walked through the slimy rioting pumpkins, she realized that something was in the distance, it was a dark figure. As she continued toward it, the slime below became more and more deep and thick as she got closer the dark figure.

As the lightning intensified, the light from it would show her flashes of the dark figure in the distance; she could see it was wearing a dark cloak, like the flashes she had when she looked into the orange black crow's eyes. But as she looked down, she could see glimpses of what she was stepping in. She stopped and looked down; as she did, a bright flash of lightning filled the clouds. Leeann became horrified by what she saw. It was blood, and she crouched down, sickened by what she saw and by what she was going to do. She reached her hand down inside the slimy blood as she felt something at her right foot. As she reached in, she moved her hand around till she could grab what she felt at her foot. It was hard, and some kind of cloth surrounded it. She pulled it up slowly out of the slimy blood; the cloth around it was soaked in the bloody slime. Leeann began to unwrap the cloth to see what was inside.

Gagging, she removed the cloth as it seemed to be a baby blanket, as she sifted through the folds and the slimy blood on it; she finally started to reveal what was hidden inside. It was a toy covered in flesh, a jack-in-the-box. Flesh hung off the box, and the handle had bloody, slimy hair hanging off it. The hair stuck around it, as if it were wrapped tightly. Leeann looked at it and tried to wipe the flesh and slimy blood off it to see what was on it. She tried to open the top, but she couldn't; she had no choice but to turn the hair raveled handle. As she put her hand on the handle, she could feel the slimy, bloody hair on it between her fingers sliding in and wrapping around her fingers.

With her face in disgust, she started to turn slowly as music started to play like an old jack-in-the-box. The music handle clinked as it turned with the sound slowly playing. Turn after slow turn, it kept going as she took in deep breaths of fear, and then it popped the lid open, startling her, making her fall back into the slimy blood as the clown popped out of the box. She took a breath out and a deep breath in as she fell, immersed in the slimy blood, dropping the jack-in-the-box back into the slimy blood. As she panicked, thrashing around in the bloody slime trying to reach the surface again, she managed to pull herself out of the slimy bloody tomb of liquid, sitting up with flesh and slimy blood hanging off of her hair and body. She let out a gasp of air and used both hands to try and wipe the flesh and slimy blood off her face, panicking.

Leeann cleared her face enough to see, but what she saw was something in front of her; she couldn't see it clearly, but enough to see a figure. She felt its breath; it was cold, and it stank like death. As she could see more clearly, it became clear that it was the figure she had seen in the distance, as she walked through the slime. She couldn't make out the face as the cloak was hanging in front of it, but she could feel its breath and smell it. Leeann was face to face with what she knew was coming for Frey and herself; she didn't know for sure, but she could feel it was.

"Who are you?"

She whispered to it. No answer was given; it just snarled and breathed in and out its cold death breath.

"What do you want from me?"

Still no answer as it leaned in closer to her and sniffed her left side like it was sniffing a well-done steak freshly cooked. Leeann didn't move but sat in fear as it then moved to her right, snarling and drooling. It sniffed her right side and quickly moved back to her face. Inches in front of her, Leeann breathed in deep with fear.

"What do you want with me and my daughter?"

The creature stopped drooling and breathed more slowly. It took its right hand and slowly lifted its pointer finger, extending it out to a point. Its black finger and long nail touched Leeann's chest, pointing straight to her heart. Leeann could feel the coldness coming through her skin and into her lungs and heart

"You want my heart?" she asked.

It began to move its finger down to Leeann's stomach and slowly put its other long fingers out and rested its hands on her belly. Leeann could feel its freezing palm on her belly as the creature moved her hand in a circular motion to the right around Leeann's belly as it started to drool and snarl, almost like a laugh.

"You can't have her, you will never have her."

The creature let out a deep groan and stopped rubbing on Leeann's belly. Then it seized her by the neck and hoisted her upright, bringing her face to face with it. Slowly, it began twisting Leeann's neck to the right, sniffing her intently—up and down—snarling and drooling all the while. It then did the same on the left side, as if preparing to devour her. Leeann breathed in fear and started to cry.

"WHAT DO YOU WANT FROM ME?" Leeann said loudly.

"WHAT DO YOU WANT WITH MY BABY?" Leeann shouted louder.

The creature sniffed left to right, right to left, up and down Leeann's neck.

"YOU CAN'T HAVE HER! YOU WON'T GET HER; YOU CAN'T HAVE ME! YOU WILL NEVER HAVE ANY OF US! WHAT THE FUCK DO YOU WANT?"

The creature stopped and released Leeann's neck. Leeann took a deep breath in and catching her breath, she broke down.

"What do you want? What do you want from me? What is it?"

As she looked down at the ground.

"What do you want?"

Leeann was crying, her breaths coming in slow, uneven waves.

"Leeann." The creature muttered. Leeann recognized that voice as she looked up slowly, the creature still covered and faceless.

"Mom?" Leeann muttered. She could never forget her mother's voice.

"Leeann, wipe your tears away."

Leeann was taken aback at the voice coming out of the creature.

"Mom, is that you?" She started to question her sanity and what had just occurred.

"Mom?"

Leeann couldn't understand what was happening, how could her mom's voice come from something so vile, so evil, and cold?

"Yes, Leeann, it's me, Mom."

Leeann couldn't believe what she was hearing. "But, how, why, why are you doing this to me?"

"Leeann, it's time for our family to be reunited. You left me to die in the cold that night."

Leeann shook her head. "No, I didn't, Mom. You walked out into that snow and left me there."

"No, Leeann." The voice began to get deeper. "You left me out there so cold, you left me to freeze and die."

"No Mom, you left me there alone, you left me, I begged you to stay."

Leeann carried the weight of that night for years, never letting go of the guilt, always believing she could have done more. But what more could she have done? She was so young, she couldn't understand what happened and why it was happening that night.

"No."

The creature snarled, "You. Left. Me."

It grabbed Leeann's throat again and squeezed, lifting Leeann into the air over her head. The creature looked up at her, exposing her face. Leeann was shocked that the face staring back at her was her mother's.

Leeann choked, "Mom—mom! Mom, why?"

The creature looked at her. "I want my babies back; you let me die". With that, the creature dropped Leeann to the ground below.

Leeann woke to see Frey next to her and the crow staring back at her from the windowsill. She got up and walked into the bathroom and turning the lights on as she entered. She looked into the mirror and then turned the water on, splashing her face with water over and over. She thought to herself, was this all a dream, was that vile creature really her mother, questioning all she had seen. As she looked up at the mirror, she saw nothing but her face, but as she looked closer, she could see the markings on her neck, the markings of that creature's hand. She didn't know what to think. It was real, all of this was real. What did her mother want with her and Frey, and when was she coming for them?

She splashed more water on her face and looked again into the mirror, and the creature's hand marks were gone. There was nothing there. She turned her head from left to right—everything was gone. Was she losing her mind, just like that night when her mother walked out into the snow and never returned? The storm outside mirrored that night, stirring memories she had buried deep beneath the silence. She couldn't help but think about what she saw, what her mother saw. Was this something that happened to the women in her family? Was this going to happen to Frey?

As Leeann collected herself, she dried her face and walked out, shutting the bathroom light off behind her, and took a glance at the crow peering out the window. The crow looked back at her, and Leeann looked back at it. "What does it want?" she whispered, knowing the crow couldn't give her the answers that she was looking for. Leeann walked over to the bed and sat down next to Frey and wondered what fate had in store for her and Frey, and whether she was prepared for what was to come.

The winter snow kept coming down, and the wind in the forest hills began to swoop across and through the dense woods. The black crow and the creature with a woman's body stood at the foundation where they were born. They were on the edge of the foundation wall, waiting for something. The creature hummed a melody as it used an old knife sitting on the foundation wall to cut a rotting apple in its hand.

Maggots crawled around the rotting apple as the creature cut slivers off, eating the maggots and the rot of the apple, drooling with each bite it took. As the winds blew, the creature stopped just before it was about to take another maggot-infested, rotting sliver of the apple. Within the wind, the creature seemed to hear a voice that gave it directions. A glow began to come from the resting ground it was born from, as black oozing oil, like liquid, began to seep out of the ground.

The light coming out was like a black light with a purple tint. The black crow began to caw into the air as the creature set down the old knife and began to stand, putting the maggot-infested apple down on the foundation wall. It turned and looked at its old resting place and snarled with drool coming out of it. The black crow flew to its shoulder and landed on it as the creature began its long walk toward the town.

Though the dense woods it walked, bringing the cold with its humming melody through the woods and past the old hermit's house, lifeless and uninhabited by any form of life.  As it traveled past the hermit's house, the wind and snow killed everything in its path, freezing deer, rabbits, and other birds. The other black crows followed from every leafless tree throughout the forest. Pine trees lost every needle that they had on each branch, as the world around began to freeze with every step the creature took through the snow. The creature stayed its course, focusing and humming its melody toward the unknowing town.

The children and parents slept in their beds, trying to stay warm as the temperature dropped lower and lower, as the wind and snow got more intense, rattling the windows throughout every house in town as the creature got closer and closer to the town below. Windows began to frost over, and ice formed on the outside. The creature was approaching quickly.

The creature approached the outskirts of the town as the winds, snow, cold, and crows above entered the town's life. As the creature entered town, the black and orange crow cawed, grabbing Leeann's attention. She knew the crow knew something. The sky filled with the darkness of black crows flying below the clouds, cawing as they entered the town.

The crows began their descent into the town, landing on each house's windowsill. As they landed, all of the parents started to fall deeper into sleep. As the creature walked the blindingly snowy streets, the streetlights began to freeze and flicker. The snow that once fell white began to fall black, like soot, just like in Leeann's vision.

The creature stopped and sniffed the air, as the black soot snow covered the white snow that had fallen since earlier that evening, shutting the town down early. The crows, still seated upon windowsills throughout the town, gazed into windows; the creature could see through all their eyes as it sniffed the air, like a dog latching onto a scent. It snarled and drooled, as if it tasted a sweet treat. It could smell and almost taste all the children within the town; it was hungry, and the town had more children than it needed. The creature was about to feast on the innocent children of the town.

Leeann lay there watching the black and orange crow start to move its head around like it could hear something in the distance. But what it heard was just outside their door. The crow turned to look at Frey and Leeann lying on the bed, while Sandy lay on the couch nearby. Leeann knew that something was here, and it was coming for them, and more importantly, Frey.

The creature walked down Homeyer Road, sniffing the air with its blood-red eyes, a crow perched upon its shoulder. The black soot snow started to fall lightly as the creature stalked its prey. The creature sniffed the air, smelling for something innocent; their essence was much more, sweeter and filling. The innocent tasted ripe and almost perfect. As the creature stopped in front of an old white house with a stone driveway, it gave a strong sniff in the air. It snarled and drooled more heavily. The creature turned and stared down the driveway, and the black crow cawed as the creature took a step from pavement to gravel with its right foot, then its left foot followed. Down the gravel driveway it walked, closer and closer to the front steps. It stopped for a second at the steps as drool dripped from its black, dead lips. It sniffed the air one more time as it began its ascent up the first of three steps to the front door. Step after step, right foot left, right foot left, to the small porch landing as it stood there in front of the white door.

The creature then extended its left arm out and placed its hand on the door; it closed its eyes and started to feel the happiness within the house. The laughter of a child, a boy who giggled at his mother and father. The innocence was so young; the child was no more than 2 years old, just learning to walk, mom and dad's first child. It could feel the mother's happiness of finally after years of trying and doctors saying she was unable to have a child, and finally having one.

Dad has his boy to carry on the family name, to take to baseball games, and to play football in the yard. The creature could sense the happiness and love that this child had and what it meant to its parents. The boy's innocence was so, the love and happiness were so delightful and so much craving, and this child was a fulfilling treat for the creature.

The crow cawed as the creature opened its eyes. The door began to freeze as the creature's hand became colder and colder. As the creature's eyes became glazed over, white snow began to fall within its icy, globed eyes. The cracks in the wood of the white door started to form as the snow in the creature's eyes intensified. The creature drooled more profusely as the pieces of the door started to fall inward onto the doormat inside, which read "Welcome To Our Home," shattering on the doormat like glass. The hole in the door widened as loose fragments gave way. The creature pushed gently, but it was enough; one by one, the splintered pieces tumbled to the doormat, shattering as they landed. The creature's eyes began to turn back to their normal black as the black crow cawed. The wind entered the home, bringing in the black soot snow with it. The creature took one step in with its right foot, followed by its left on the doormat, as a crunch from under its bare feet crushed the pieces from the door that had fallen.

The creature's eyes rolled back into its head as it lifted its head into the air and sniffed the air, grunting and groaning as it searched for the direction of its prey. The black crow flew off the creature's shoulder and flew up the steps in front of them, landing on the railing post. The creature stopped and its eyes rolled back to normal, slowly raising its head up to look up the steps. The crow cawed. Right foot first, then left, as it scaled the steps one foot in front of another, creeping slowly up the steps, the steps creaking with each step. Then the creature stopped in front of a photograph on its left.

It lifted its left arm and opened its hand, placing it on the photograph, and began to move its hand across it, as if petting it. It never turned its head, as if it liked the feeling of the photograph, as if it was taking it in through the palm of its hand. The photograph was of the mother wearing her red blouse with her brown hair tied back into a bun, holding their newborn son in a blue swaddle blanket sitting on the couch and the father sitting next to her in gray sweater and a white dress shirt underneath with his arm around his loving wife both head-to-head looking down at their newborn with the dads finger being held by his little boy. The smiles on their faces were filled with hope and love for their boy and one another.

The creature then took its nails and scratched them down the photograph, leaving the photograph with shreds and tears. The creature continued its walk up the steps to find its prey. It reached the top of the steps and looked to its right, down a long hallway with three doors: one to the right, one to the left, and another at the end of the hallway. The creature turned and started its walk down the hallway. As it started walking, the black crow flew to its right shoulder and perched upon it with its red bloodshot eyes moving from left to right.

As they reached the first door on the left, the creature stopped and extended its left hand, creaking open the door with just a slight push, as it was not fully closed. The black crow flew in and flew around the room. It was a nursery, but it was still being set up; the baby's crib was up and covered in plastic, as was the oak-stained dresser. The walls were half-painted blue, with plastic on the floor near the walls to prevent paint from getting on the floor from drips. The crow flew back and to the creature's left shoulder this time. As they continued down the hall to the next door on the right, the creature heard a whimpering coming from the door at the end of the hall. The creature stopped and smelled the air, lifting its head into the sky. It could smell the baby's breath as it whimpered; the black crow kept its blood-red eyes fixed on the door at the end of the hall.

They continued down the hall as the creature could smell more and more of the baby's breath and the baby's innocent flesh. The door at the end of the hallway was cracked open just a little. The creature reached out its right arm and put its open hand on the door, and slowly pushed it open. The door creaked as it opened slowly to reveal a large wooden post bed, with red sheets and a thick red blanket, on which the man and the woman slept soundly underneath both the sheet and blanket. The creature heard the baby's whimper again and turned toward the window on the left side of the room. There, bathed in the faint light beneath the glass, lay its prey.

The little baby boy lay there all snug in his old wooden crib, snuggled up with his blue blanket and his stuffed animals. His crib mobile dangled above, with elephants, giraffes, and monkeys hanging from it. He had his crib bumpers, and he was wearing his father's and mother's favorite pajamas, his blue flannel shirt, and pants. The little boy shivered a bit from the cold that slowly filled the room as the creature opened the door, from the draft coming up the steps from the house door downstairs.

The crow flew to the headboard as the husband and wife lay there, the woman on the left facing the baby's crib and the man facing the same way, with one arm around his wife, holding her tightly under the red blanket. The creature slowly walked over to the baby's crib right foot first, followed by the left, as the coldness filled the room with each creaking step it took. As it approached the baby's crib, it grumbled in delight and drooled more and more as it could taste the baby boy's life inside, and it could hear his little heartbeat.

As the creature crept up to the crib, the little boy started to whimper more and more because it became colder and colder in the room. As the creature looked into the crib and stood next to it in front of the window, it gazed outside through the glass for a moment, the town growing darker with every drop of black soot snow falling from the dense clouds. It turned around slowly and looked into the crib as the baby whimpered more and more loudly, with the cold now consuming the room. It reached down with both of its long, black, fingered nails, wrapping the blue blanket around the baby in the crib, and scooped the baby up, slowly lifting it to its chest. The creature started humming a melody as it turned back to the window and gazed out into the town, as it started to become more covered in the falling black snow.

The baby began to whimper more as the creature hummed the melody; the creature held the baby with one hand while moving the other and used it to rub the baby's head. As it touched the baby's skin, the baby began to feel the chill and started to whine, and then cry. The creature hummed the melody louder. The mother started to move around as she could hear in her deep sleep that the baby was starting to whine and whine louder. She could also hear the humming melody get louder. As she opened her eyes, she could see the creature holding her son.

"Bill, Bill, get up."

Bill started to wake up, but his eyes were not fully open, "What, what is it, Nikki?"

Bill opened his eyes, "What the…?"

The creature looked at them, holding their son in its arms.

"Please, please, put the baby down."

Nikki pleaded with the creature.

"Who are you? Put my son down, now!"

Bill yelled as he was about to get out of bed, "Give me my son."

As Bill started to get up, the creature raised its hand, which it rubbed across the baby's head. Bill and Nikki couldn't move, but they could still speak.

"What are you? Please give me my boy."

Nikki pleaded as she tried to cry, but her tears turned to ice, freezing her eyes open and her tears to her cheeks. Bill couldn't move or speak at all, and he couldn't blink, either, so all they could do was watch in horror.

As the baby began to cry, the creature stopped its melody and stared into the baby's eyes. The baby's lips started to turn blue as its skin started to turn pale, as white as a porcelain doll. The baby's lungs started to freeze as it could no longer cry. The creature stared deep into the baby's blue eyes as the baby could see the blackness as a gaze filled its eyes, and then snow began to fall within. The baby's spine started to freeze, as did every bone in its body. The baby's spine started to crack, as the baby lay there in pain, but unable to move. As the baby's spine started to crack, so did the other bones within its body.

The creature stared deeper and deeper until it could absorb what it needed. The creature's chest began to glow a deep red through its black skin, a pulsating glow that emanated from within. The baby's life was slipping away as its skin started to crack and tear away, blood oozing out, the baby's spine shattered into sharp pieces of glass, cutting through its back like razor blades, breaking through the already cracking, oozing blood. The baby's eyes started to crack as the last of its life disappeared out of its body. The glowing of the creature's chest dimmed to nothing. The creature looked into the eyes of the mother and father as it crushed their lifeless baby boy's body to nothing and dropped it on the floor, shattering it into pieces.

The mother and father could feel the pain of their son's death through the gaze of the creature's eyes. The black crow then flew down to the creature's left shoulder and stared into the eyes of Bill and Nikki with its blood-red eyes. As the crow cocked his head to the left and right, slowly, Bill and Nikki could feel it digging into their eyes and in to their brains. The crow started to move its head faster side to side. Bill and Nikki's eyes started to bleed as the crow moved its head back and forth, faster and faster. It dug deeper and deeper into their brains; they could feel it digging and digging like a spoon, just digging and digging. Their eyes bleed and bleed until they bleed out chunks of their brains through their eyes.

As the creature walked out of the room, the cold followed. Bill and Nikki's bodies unfroze and lay there in their own blood and brains. Their son lay on the floor in a puddle of his own flesh, blood, and shattered pieces of bones, like chunky tomato soup with sprinkles of salt.

Leeann drifted off to sleep as she stared into the black, orange crow's eyes. As the crow stood looking at Leeann and Frey sleeping, Frey woke up with her eyes opening quickly and wide as she let out a blistering cry of a scream. Jolting them both awake, Leeann and Sandy instantly woke up. Sandy jumped up so quick to see what was happening. Leeann looked directly at the window as her eyes opened, but only caught a glance at what was outside. As she looked at Frey screaming and Sandy came over from off the couch

"What's happening?"

Leeann picked Frey up, and she was screaming and crying, "I don't know. Frey, baby, calm down. Honey, calm down."

Sandy started to panic, "Frey, it's okay, Frey baby."

The creature could hear Frey's screams as it walked down the steps from Bill and Nikki's house. It stopped and stared out the broken front door. The echo of Frey's screams filled the already quiet town covered in darkness. The creature looked at the black crow on its left shoulder. The black crow took flight, gliding down the remaining steps before soaring into the air, drawn toward the source of the scream.

Leeann walked around the room holding Frey as she cried and screamed. It's like she was in pain. Leeann couldn't figure out what happened. Was it a nightmare? What was going on? She looked to the black and orange crow for guidance.

"Can you please help her?"

The black and orange crow just looked at her and tilted its head at her.

"Please."

Leeann laid Frey back on the bed as she continued to cry and scream, "Please!"

As she looked at the black and orange crow, the crow flew over to the bed and tried to help soothe Frey and calm her down, but nothing worked. Frey cried and screamed over and over, starting to fuss and violently thrash her body.

Then she stopped and looked out the window. Leeann looked to see, as did the black and orange crow and Sandy. On the outside of the windowsill, there stood the black blood-red-eyed crow staring back at them. Frey stared into its red eyes, and Leeann did as well. Sandy noticed the crow but stared out further past it and saw the black soot snow.

"What the hell, black snow?" Sandy muttered

As Leeann started to feel her eyes start to water, she seemed to be losing sight in her eyes; she could only see blurs. Frey starred at the black crows eye's and the black and orange crow cawed, the black crow cawed back, then Frey's eyes started to turn orange colored the black crow cawed loudly over and over as it flew away to the roof top of Leeann's building and cawed and cawed, bringing all the other crows to the building as they left the windowsills of all other buildings they were sitting on. They all stood on the building cawing.

Sandy looked over at Leeann, "Oh, my God, Leeann, your eyes are bleeding."

Leeann wiped away the blood, but still couldn't see clearly. "My eyes are what?"

Sandy rushed to the bathroom and grabbed a rag from the bath towel rack, and ran it under water.

"Your eyes are bleeding, Leeann."

Sandy rushed over to her with the wet rag and put it on Leeann's eyes.

"Hold this here, I'll be right back".

Leeann held the rag on her eyes; she couldn't understand what was going on. Sandy rushed under the kitchen sink to grab the medical kit. Frey looked at her mother, as did the black and orange crow. Sandy came back and sat next to Leeann.

"Let me take the rag off your face."

As she did, she saw nothing there; the blood was gone, but Leeann still could see nothing at all. Sandy looked into Leeann's eyes as they started to cloud over.

"Leeann, what is happening?"

Leeann didn't know that all she could do was try to cry, but nothing would come out, no tears, nothing.

"I don't know Sandy, I don't know."

As she broke down, shedding no tears.

The creature could hear the crows cawing, and it continued down the steps and out the door. It entered and followed the crows' caws.

Leeann gathered herself together.

"Sandy, I need you to be my eyes for me."

Sandy looked at Leeann's white eyes and was about to break out into tears.

"Ok, what do you need?"

Leeann searched for Sandy's hand and searched for it, and once she found it, she held her hand.

"Sandy, I love you, and I need you to be strong for me and for Frey. I need you to be my eyes. I believe something is coming for us, and that red-eyed crow was its guardian. Just listen, they're all on the roof and they're calling for something".

Sandy listened and could hear them cawing.

"I can hear them. What do you need me to do?"

Leeann was still holding Sandy's hand.

"Make sure it doesn't get Frey, protect her, please".

Sandy looked down at Leeann's hand on hers.

"I always will."

"Thank you," Leeann said with a smile. "Thank you."

The creature continued to follow the lead of the crow's caws echoing through the dead streets of the town. The black soot snow fell from the sky as the creature walked down Main Street. As the creature walked past Thompson's Candy and old man Johnson's Liquor, it could feel that something was inside Grady's Pizza Joint, and it was a powerful soul. The crows flocked and stood on top of Grady's, cawing high in the sky. The red-eyed crow flew down to the creature's right shoulder as it cawed, seeming to talk to the creature as it stopped at Grady's front door.

Leeann seemed to know it was there. She lost her sight due to blurred vision, but her hearing seemed to be fine.

"What is it, Leeann?" Sandy had noticed Leeann was facing the apartment door.

"It's here, I can feel it, we need to protect Frey."

The black and orange crow could feel it too as it lay down next to Frey. Frey's eyes were wide open as she looked at the crow's eyes, as they seemed to communicate through their eyes. The crow cawed as if to tell Leeann danger was in the air.

"Sandy?" She walked over to Leeann.

"I'm here."

"Sandy, I need you to take Frey into the other rotom," Leeann whispered to Sandy.

"Ok, I will".

"Please keep her in there and safe. Do not come out of that room, no matter what."

"But, Leeann?"

"Just don't, please, no matter what. Promise me?" Leeann begged.

"Ok, Leeann, I won't."

She picked up Frey and walked into the other room.

"You go too," Leeann said to the crow.

The crow cawed at Leeann and flew to her left shoulder.

"Go, please."

The crow cawed again and stood on her shoulder as if in defiance.

"Ok, Sandy, shut the door." Sandy did just that.

"You are going to protect her here with me, aren't you?"

The crow cawed as it answered yes, both of them standing there facing the door.

The creature waited at the door and waited till the black, red-eyed crow and the black crows above stopped cawing. Silence filled the town. The creature lifted its right arm and placed its hand on the door of Grady's. Its eyes started to get a white gaze, floating inside its blackness as the door began to freeze over. The glass on the top of the door started to frost and crack like thin ice on a pond. The creature took a breath in and exhaled a cold breath out as it slowly pushed in on the door cracking the wood below and shattering the frosted glass above to the floor inside Grady's. The cracking wood started to splinter and break down inside the shop, joining the frosted glass. The creature brought its arm slowly back to its side, and it took a step in with its right foot, stepping down barefoot on the shattered glass and splintered wood lying on the floor as it raised its head to sniff the air for its prey.

Leeann and the crow heard the glass hitting the floor downstairs, knowing it was there. The creature lifted its head into the air and, from left to right, sniffed the air, as if it were a dog looking for food. It walked through the shop very slowly, sniffing left to right, walking through the eating area, and to the back of the counter, passing the ovens. Then it stopped like it smelled what it was looking for, at the back door. It looked forward, sniffed in a deep smell, and then grinned at the door. The drool started to run from its lips down to the floor. Then it reached out with its left arm, extended its black hand, fingers out, and took a swipe with its long nails at the door, clawing the wood as it splintered under its nails. Then it swiped again with the same arm and black claw-like nails, shoving more wood splinters under its nails. The nail marks were deep into the wood, as the creature put the palm of its hand on the scratched door and pushed it with a hard shove, sending shards of wood flying onto the steps on the other side of the door that lead up to Leeann's apartment.

The black, red-eyed crow and the creature took a step onto the landing, one foot in front of the other stepping on the shattered pieces of the wooden door scattered all over the landing and the first few steps. With each step, the splinters pierced through its black feet as it slowly crept up the steps, right foot then left foot repeat till it reached the top landing. As it turned to the only door, Leeann could feel its presence outside the door, with every step closer the creature brought with it coldness and the smell of death in the air, and Leeann could feel the chill down her spine. The creature took four steps, right foot left to the door of Leeann's apartment, and extended its right arm out and pointed its pointer finger out with its long nail just a hair away from touching the door. Leeann could hear it breathing outside the apartment door.

As the creature's nail touched the door, with the cloudy gaze still swirling in its back eyes, the black, red-eyed crow cawed. The crows on the top of the building flew off of the roof and started to fly left in a circle around the building, swirling the black soot snow with them. Leeann could hear the crows, and she seemed to be able to feel them as well.

The creature began to move its nail up the wooden door and slowly brought it down, carving a deep, splintered scratch within it straight down the middle down to the floor. The sound was like nails on a chalkboard piercing through Leeann's ears. The creature then put its palm on the middle of the door and pushed so slightly, breaking it in, the hinge part still attached to the frame, and the other side of the door flying across the room. Leeann crouched down as she heard the door crack apart, covering her face with both hands, and the black and orange crow hung onto her shoulder.

As the creature stood in the doorway before taking a step, the black, red-eyed crow cawed. Leeann uncovered her face and slowly stood up, facing the doorway as the black, orange crow cawed back, staring into the black, red-eyed crow's eyes. The creature drooled and groaned as it took a step into the apartment. Leeann could feel each step of the creature's feet through the floor, and feel the coldness getting closer. She could see a blurry shadow of it approaching her, and all she could do was stand there waiting.

The creature stopped within inches of Leeann; they were almost nose to nose. Leeann could feel its cold breath on her face as it breathed on her. The crows stared at one another as they were waiting for orders to attack one another.

"What do you want from me?"

The creature snarled at Leeann as Leeann stood her ground.

"What do you want from me?"

Again, the creature just snarled at her. Leeann became frustrated

"WHAT THE FUCK DO YOU WANT FROM ME!?" Leeann yelled. As she slapped the creature across the face with her right hand, the creature's head moved slightly, and then it snarled more and more. Leeann then yelled again…

"WHAT THE FUCK DO YOU…"

The creature grabbed Leeann's neck and lifted her up in the air, as the black and orange crow attempted to lunge at the creature's face, the black, red-eyed crow then lunged at the black and orange crow as they both fell to the ground, attacking one another. As the creature held Leeann in the air, Leeann could feel the coldness in her throat, she felt fear and the creature turned Leeann's head to the left and sniffed up the side of her neck and then turned Leeann's head to the right and sniffed up that side as well, snarling and drool dripping down its lip to the floor below. Then it ran its slimy tongue up the right side of Leeann's face before turning her head forward.

Sandy could hear the noise outside the door and the crows fighting as they rolled around on the floor. She tried to stay silent as she could hear all this, and as she held Frey, Frey became increasingly fidgety; she couldn't stay still, which was making her irritable. Frey started to whine quietly, but Sandy didn't know how long Frey would stay quiet.

The creature could hear Frey's quiet whines and stopped running its slimy tongue up the side of Leeann's face and threw Leeann to the ground. As Leeann hit the ground, trying to catch her breath, the creature began walking to the door where Sandy and Frey were. Leeann tried to yell to Sandy that it was coming, but she couldn't catch her breath, and her throat was frozen from the creature's cold hand being wrapped around it.

The black and orange crow tried to break away from the black, red-eyed crow as they fought on the floor, rolling around. As Leeann caught her breath enough to yell, the black, red-eyed crow broke away from the black and orange crow and flew to Leeann's face, clawing and pecking at her. As it scratched and clawed at her flesh, Leeann tried to fight it off by grabbing it, but it pecked and bit at her. The black and orange crow flew to the aggressor, trying to scratch, claw, and peck at its face. But as it did, the creature grabbed the black and orange crow and, with its icy, frozen hands, sent the coldness through its body, throwing it to the floor.

The creature put its left cold hand up, and before even touching the door, the door froze and shattered, breaking straight down to the ground in pieces. As Sandy held Frey in her arms, crouched down in the left corner of the room facing the wall's crease, the creature walked in. Leeann fought to keep the black, red-eyed crow from tearing more and more through her flesh, as she screamed for Frey.

The creature walked across the room as Sandy began to whimper, and Frey cried out as the coldness of the creature intensified while it approached them.

"No, please, leave us be, please," Sandy whimpered. "Please."

The creature reached down to Sandy's shoulder. Sandy could feel the coldness through her skin and into her bones; she began to shake.

"No, please, no, please, please."

Sandy started to freeze more and more as her cries were not answered, she could feel its breath on her, and she couldn't move. As the creature reached down with both hands to take Frey from Sandy's arms, Sandy held on as hard as she could, but she couldn't stop the creature from pulling Frey from her hands as she became frozen in place.

The creature smiled and drooled as it lifted Frey to its chest and cradled her in its cold, black arms. As it turned around to see Leeann still fighting off the red-eyed crow, bleeding from the scratches it inflicted upon her face. The creature walked out of the room and snarled as it looked at a crying Frey in its arms, as the creature started to hum a melody rocking Frey, the eyes of the creature began to fill more and more with the white haze inside of its blackened eyes, the snow began to fall within the haze. Frey looked into the creature's eyes, which were blue, dark, cold, and frozen.

Frey's body began to freeze as her lips turned blue and her bones started to freeze. Frey took a breath and then another as her breath was cold. Frey took one last breath as her skin began to crack like an old porcelain doll, her eyes frosted over as she breathed her last breath out. Leeann could feel her daughter's life fading out of her as she fought the crow off enough to cover her head as she lay it down on the floor

"Frey baby, Frey, no!!!" Leeann cried out, "Come back to mommy, please, no Frey!"

The creature held Frey's lifeless body as Frey's body started to break into pieces with every crack of her skin, becoming more and more fragile. The creature snarled and smiled as the first piece of Frey fell to the ground.

But underneath the first piece, there lay another brighter piece, a piece of warm skin. Another piece fell as more and more of the frozen skin fell. But underneath it all was brighter and warmer skin as Frey's body seemed to be shedding the frozen skin off and revealing new, living, warm skin. Her bones began to warm and repair themselves. The creature couldn't believe what it was seeing; it tried to let go and drop Frey, but it couldn't.

Frey's eyes began to shift from their blue, dark, and cold hue to a glowing orange as Frey took in a deep breath. The creature couldn't look away as Frey stared into its eyes, warming the creature from the inside out. The black, red-eyed crow cawed as Leeann reached out and grabbed it and held it. She lifted her head up and could see clearly as Frey lit up into a fire-like gaze; she was so bright.

The creature started to burn from the inside out as it started to melt. Sandy was able to move and ran out into the room; she could see that the scratches and tears on her face were gone too, the creature was melting. Just as the creature was about to drop Frey, Sandy grabbed her in her arms as the creature began to strip off its rags and melt, stumbling throughout the apartment. The crows circling the outside of the building started to scatter into the air and disappear. The black soot snow became white again.

As the creature turned to look at Leeann now holding a rotting pumpkin in her hands where the black, red-eyed crow once was, the creature took one deep breath and its eyes rolled out of its head and onto the floor, rolling like marbles do across to the black and orange crow laying unfrozen on the floor not breathing.

Leeann ran to Sandy and took Frey in her arms. She couldn't help but cry as she held baby Frey in her arms.

"Oh my God, my baby, Frey! I thought I lost you, I thought you were gone, my baby girl!"

Leeann looked into Frey's eyes; Frey's eyes were such a bright orange she couldn't believe it. But as Frey stared into Leeann's eyes, she saw that they dimmed to a darker orange, and it also told her to bring Frey to the black and orange crow. Leeann knew that Frey needed the crow as her protector. She walked over to the crow's body, picked it up, and walked over to the bed. She laid Frey and the crow down together at Frey's chest and covered them up. Leeann turned around to walk over to Sandy and give her a hug.

"Thank you, so much, thank you, Sandy.", Leeann whispered as she wrapped her arm around her friend's shoulder.

Sandy looked over Leeann's shoulder.

"Look, Leeann."

Leeann turned around; the black and orange crow was alive and lying right next to Frey. The black and orange crow looked at Leeann.

"I know, I know."

"It had been 18 years since that night. I can still feel the cold darkness within that creature's eyes. My mother continued to raise me in this town with my Aunt, Sandy, and Uncle, Grady. My mother took over Grady's Pizza Joint from Uncle Grady when he retired, but he is always there, as if he still owns the place, still teasing my mother. Aunt Sandy still comes over every day and hangs out with us. Nothing really is said about that night 18 years ago, but you can tell mom really is still cautious about the world around her. I never knew how I got here without a father, and I will someday find out why and how I got here, but until then, I will live my life. The orange and black crow we now call Leona Ann is still here, watching over me and my mom. I know later on I will be taking a drive into the mountains; something is pulling me there."

Frey knew that it was going to come to this day. She got dressed, threw on her black sports bra, an old flannel with the sleeves cut off, and her short shorts. She walked out of the pizza joint, kissed her mother goodbye, and headed out the door. As she got into the car and drove off, Leona Ann flew above her, leading the way into the mountains. People were enjoying the nice July weather and biking and walking up and down Main Street.

As Frey drove up and out of town into the mountains, she didn't see much; she followed Leona Ann as she flew above. As the day warmed, Frey pulled over near the old pine trees and parked as Leona Ann landed on an old pine branch.

She cawed, and Frey got out of the car carrying her backpack with something in it.

Frey walked through the wooded pines and up to an old foundation, where Leona Ann had landed. As she approached it, she could feel a connection to it. Two little girls came running up wearing sun dresses and walked up to Frey.

"What are you two little ones doing out here?"

The little girl with the blond hair looked at Frey and said, "We both heard a melody coming from here."

Frey smiled and spoke, "Maybe it was the birds chirping that sounded like a melody".

The brown-haired girl looked at her and giggled.

"Birds don't hum a melody."

Frey smiled and said, "Yes, they do." But she knew it was what she was carrying in the pack she had bought that was carrying the melody that the little girls heard.

The little girls could hear their mother calling for them in the distance.

Frey smiled, "Now run along, mommy is calling for you."

The little girls smiled and ran off giggling into the distance, "Coming, Mom!"

As Frey reached into her bag and pulled out a wooden box, she slowly opened it and pulled out the creature's eyes her mother collected that night, and held them in her hands as Leona Ann watched. Frey scanned over the land with them in her hand, rolling them around like Baoding Balls. She scanned the ground around the foundation as the eyes hummed a melody. As she did, her eyes began to feel hot, then cold, then hot again, then finally colder as she reached the exact spot where the creature was born. As Frey rolled the eyes around in her hand, she could see the deep ground starting to pull something from the ground to the surface. As she moved around the dirt, she found something shiny just under the dirt.

As she pulled it up, she realized it was an oddly jagged-shaped amulet that had these markings on it that looked like ancient letters that she couldn't quite understand. It seemed to be a piece, as it appeared to have been broken off from many others. As she put it in her pocket, she set the eyes back in the box and pulled the creature's cloak from her bag, all tattered and torn. She brought it back to the place where she had found the emblem and laid it down on the ground. She reached into the sack again and pulled out a match. She skimmed it across a rock, lighting it, and lit the cloth on fire, as blue, cold flames burned it to ash. Frey stood up and watched it burn. As it did, Frey opened up the box with the eyes still humming a melody, she then pulled them out one by one and put them in her mouth and chewed them, swallowing each chunk as they went down.

As she walked away with her pack in hand and Leona Ann on her right shoulder, she looked back and then to the amulet in her left hand. She knew this was the beginning of something far greater. She knew eating the eyes was the only way to stop the birth of evil, which changed her left eye to white like winter snow.

"To stop evil, you must consume evil," she whispered as she walked back to her car.

As she got in her car and Leona Ann sat on her shoulder, she started the engine and began driving back down the hill. As she drove over a hill, she saw a man walking a dog on the side of the road toward her. She didn't understand how she didn't pass the man coming up to the mountains, but she pulled alongside him and stopped.

"Hey, are you ok?"

The man wearing a black T-shirt and jeans looked at her with his brown eyes and black, wavy, thinning hair, "Yeah, I'm ok, just taking my dog for a walk."

Frey saw that the dog looked tired and old; it was a long-haired lab. She smiled, "Do you want a ride? Your dog looks beat and in need of water."

The man smiled, "Oh, Taz, no, he's ok."

Frey looked at him and reached behind her, handing him two bottles of water she had in a cooler behind the passenger seat for him and the dog.

The man took the bottled water.

"Thank you..." He paused.

"Oh, sorry, my name is Frey," she said

The man smiled at her and spoke. "Thank you, Frey. My name is Anthony, but people call me by my first name, Brian."

Frey smiled back. "Well, I'll see you around town, maybe if you come back this way again."

Brain smiled back, "You just might, thank you."

Frey drove off and held the amulet in her hands, and turned the radio on. As she looked into the rearview mirror, hanging on her windshield, she could see the man, Brian, and the dog, Taz, standing on the side of the road, staring at her from a distance. Frey pulled over, keeping the car running. Brian looked down at Taz as he began to whine and said,

"Don't worry, buddy, we'll see her again. But we need to find the others.

Frey was confused and looked back through her back window. Brian and Taz were gone. Like they were never there..